HER SHAMEFUL SECRET

BY
SUSANNA CARR

MILLS &
BOON

All the characters in this book have no existence outside the imagination
of the author, and have no relation whatsoever to anyone bearing the

CLACKMANNANSHIRE
COUNCIL

40007301F	
Bertrams	04/01/2013
CAR	£13.50
ADU	AF

First published in Great Britain 2013
by Mills & Boon, an imprint of Harlequin (UK) Limited.
Harlequin (UK) Limited, Eton House, 18-24 Paradise Road,
Richmond, Surrey TW9 1SR

© Susanna Carr 2013

ISBN: 978 0 263 23394 0

Harlequin (UK) policy is to use papers that are natural, renewable
and recyclable products and made from wood grown in sustainable
forests. The logging and manufacturing process conform to the
legal environmental regulations of the country of origin.

Printed and bound in Great Britain
by CPI Antony Rowe, Chippenham, Wiltshire

HER SHAMEFUL
SECRET

To Carly Byrne and Lucy Gilmour with thanks
for their insights and generous support.

CHAPTER ONE

ISABELLA WILLIAMS heard the throaty growl of an expensive sports car and lifted her head like a hunted animal scenting danger. The sudden move made her head spin. She took a step back, gripping the serving tray as she fought for her balance.

The sound of the car faded before she turned to see it. Isabella exhaled shakily, her bunched muscles relaxing. She swiped her hand against her clammy forehead, hating how her imagination ran wild. Her mind was playing tricks on her. One sports car drove past her and she immediately thought of him.

It was ridiculous to think that Antonio Rossi was in this part of Rome, or even searching for her. She rolled her eyes in self-disgust. She'd only shared a bed with him for a few glorious months in the spring. The guy would have long forgotten her. He was every woman's secret fantasy and Isabella was certain that she had been replaced the moment she left his bed.

The thought pricked at Isabella and she blinked away the tears that stung in the backs of her eyes. Glancing at the clock, she calculated how many more hours she had left on her shift. Too many. All she wanted to do was crawl back into bed, burrow under the threadbare covers and keep the world at bay. But she couldn't afford to take a day off. She needed every euro to survive.

"Isabella, you have customers waiting," her boss barked at her.

She simply nodded, too tired to give her usual sarcastic response, and headed toward one of the small tables on the sidewalk café. She would get through this day just like every other day. One foot in front of the other. One minute at a time.

It felt like she had waded through sludge by the time she got to the tiny table where the couple waited. They didn't seem to mind her slow pace. The man gently, almost reverently, kissed the woman's lips. Envy pierced through Isabella's stupor. She bit down on her lip to hold back a whimper as she remembered what it felt like to be adored and desired.

Isabella's shoulders slumped as the bittersweet memories poured over her. She couldn't recapture that kind of love. She would never be the center of Antonio's attention again, and he would no longer be her entire world. She missed his possessive kisses and the raw hunger they'd shared. But, much as she missed him, he would never take her back. Not when he discovered the truth.

Her knees threatened to buckle under the weight of her regret. She gritted her teeth and harnessed the last of her self-control. Those wildly romantic days were over, she reminded herself fiercely. It was best not to think of them.

"Are you ready to order?" she asked hoarsely in Italian. Her grasp of the language wasn't that great, despite her taking a few classes in college. Her struggle to communicate made it even more difficult to get through a day.

Once she'd had big dreams of becoming fluent in Italian, transforming herself into a sophisticated and glamorous woman and taking the city of Rome by storm. She'd wanted to find adventure, beauty and love. For a brief moment she'd had it all in her grasp, but she'd allowed it to slip through her fingers.

Now she worked all day in this dump and had no money. People either ignored her or viewed her as trash. So much for her transformation. She could have gotten that treatment back home. At least then she would know what was being said behind her back. She lived in a room above the café that didn't have running water or a lock on the door. All she had was the weight of the world on her shoulders and a deep need to survive.

As she took down the order and walked back to the kitchen Isabella realized that she was in danger of getting stuck here. She needed to work harder, faster and smarter if she wanted to return to America in the next few months. Now more than ever she needed to surround herself with the familiar. Find a place where she could keep her head down, work hard and complete her college degree. After all this time yearning for excitement, she now longed to find a safe haven.

But she didn't think she could keep this up, working long hours and barely getting by. And it was only going to get harder. The thought made her want to drop to the floor in a heap and cry.

Isabella leaned against the kitchen wall. One day she'd get out of this nightmare. She weakly closed her eyes, ignoring her boss's reprimand to hurry. Soon she'd have enough money to fly back to America. She'd start over and maybe get it right the next time. If there was one thing she could rely on it was learning from her mistakes.

Antonio Rossi surveyed the small sidewalk café. After searching all weekend he was going to face the woman who had almost destroyed him and his family. He strode to an empty table and sat down, his lethal grace concealing the anticipation of battle that was racing through his veins. This time he wasn't going to fall for Isabella's big blue eyes and innocent beauty. He would be in command.

He leaned back, his legs sprawled under the tiny table. Sliding dark sunglasses on his nose, Antonio looked at the paint-chipped, rusted furniture. Of all the places he'd thought she would be, he mused as he glimpsed the ratted, faded awning, he hadn't pictured a dirty little café on the wrong side of Rome.

Why was Isabella living in this filth and poverty? It didn't make sense. He had opened his world to her. She had lived in his penthouse apartment and shared his bed. She had had his servants to take care of her.

And she'd thrown it all away when she'd slept with his brother.

The knowledge still ate away at him. He had provided Isabella with everything, but it hadn't been enough. No matter how much he'd given, how hard he'd worked, he hadn't been able to compare with his brother. It had always been that way.

Still, he had been blindsided by Giovanni's drunken confession six months ago. Had responded by casting

Isabella and Giovanni out of his life. It had been swift and vicious, but they had deserved much worse.

Isabella stepped into his view. Tension gripped Antonio, and he braced himself for the emotional impact as he watched her precariously balance two cappuccinos on a serving tray. He had prepared himself for it, but seeing her was like a punch to his gut as she walked past him.

She wore a thin black T-shirt, a skimpy denim skirt and scuffed black flats, but she still had the power to draw his attention. His gaze lingered on her bare legs. He remembered how they'd felt wrapped around his hips as he drove into her welcoming body.

Antonio exhaled slowly and purged the image from his mind. He would not be distracted by her sexual allure or her innocent face. He had made the mistake of lowering his guard with her. He had trusted Isabella and got close to her. That wouldn't happen again.

Antonio grimly watched her serve the couple, noticing that she looked different. The last time he'd seen her, she had been asleep in his bed, flushed and naked, her long blonde hair fanning like a halo across the white silk pillow.

Isabella now looked pale and sickly. Her hair fell in a limp ponytail. The curves that had used to make him forget his next thought had diminished. She was bony and frail.

She looked terrible. A cruel smile flickered on the edge of his mouth. Antonio hoped she'd been to hell and back. He was prepared to take her there again.

He'd once believed she was sweet and innocent, but it had all been a lie. Her blushes and slow smiles had disarmed him and he had been convinced that she wanted only him. But her open affection had been a smoke-screen.

It turned out that Isabella was a master of the mind game and outplayed the most conniving women in his world, who would lie, cheat and bed-hop to get closer to Gio, heir to the Rossi fortune. Isabella had seduced Antonio with her angelic beauty. Made him believe that he was her first choice. Her only choice. But all that time she had been working her magic on Giovanni.

Isabella turned away from the table and headed towards him. Her head was bent as she grabbed her notepad and pen. Tension coiled inside him, ready to spring. He sat unnaturally still, refusing to make any sudden moves that would alert her to impending danger.

"Are you ready to order?" she asked uninterestedly.

Her hoarse voice was nothing like the husky whisper he remembered.

"Hello, Bella."

No, no, no!

She looked up sharply and her cloudy eyes cleared as she focused on Antonio. He was here. In front of her. Waiting for her to make the next move, even though they both knew it was useless.

Run. The word screamed through her brain.

Isabella slowly blinked. Maybe she was hallucinating. She hadn't been herself lately. There was no way Antonio Rossi, billionaire, member of the social elite, would be sitting in this café.

But her imagination couldn't conjure the electric current coursing through her body from his nearness. Or the panic that stole her breath. Her heart gave a brutal leap before it plummeted.

Does he know? Is that why he's here?

She couldn't stop staring at him like a deer caught in the headlights. Antonio wore a black pinstripe suit, the ruthlessly tailored lines emphasizing his broad shoulders and lean, muscular body. The hand-made shirt and silk tie offered a veneer of civility, but they couldn't mask his animal magnetism. He was the most sensual man she had ever known, and the most powerful.

Antonio Rossi was also the most callous person she'd met.

Isabella took short, choppy breaths, but she was suffocating with dread. She couldn't gauge his next move or his next thought. She only knew that it was going to be devastating.

She had been an idiot to get involved with him. He was the kind of man her mother had often warned her about. Antonio would see a woman like her only as a plaything and then discard her when something better came along. Isabella knew all this but she had still been drawn to him like a moth to a flame. Even now she felt the pull and she couldn't stop staring at him.

His eyes were hidden behind the sunglasses, but the angles and lines of his savagely masculine face were just as sharp and aggressive as she remembered. Antonio wasn't beautiful, but his dark, striking looks made women of all ages eager for another glimpse of him.

Run. And don't look back.

"Antonio?" Her voice was high and reedy. "What are you doing here?"

"I've come for you."

She shivered. She'd never thought she would see him again or hear those words. But it was too late. She couldn't go back. She wouldn't let herself think that it was possible. "Why?"

"Why?" Antonio leaned back in his chair and arrogantly studied her appearance.

Her skin tingled as she felt his lazy gaze sliding over her tired body and cheap clothes. Her pulse tripped before galloping at maximum speed. *How much did he know?*

She couldn't tell because his sunglasses hid his eyes. Was he here because he missed the sex? What they had shared had been hot, raw and primitive. It had made her wild, irresponsible and addicted to him. When they were together nothing else had mattered. And if she were smart she would keep her distance before she fell under his spell again.

Her muscles were locked, her feet were still, but her heart pounded hard against her ribs. She should tell him to leave and then get as far away as she could, but instead she was letting him take a good, long look at her.

"You need to leave. Now." She forced the words out. She needed to be harsh. In the end it would be kinder this way.

"Bella…" he warned in a low growl.

Only Antonio called her that. She'd used to love hearing him say it with a hint of a smile when he greeted her, or in awe as she brought him satisfaction with her mouth. Now, hearing him say it again, this time in anger, it brought a pang in her heart.

"I have nothing to say to you," she said in a rush.

His face hardened with displeasure. Antonio whipped off his dark sunglasses and glared at her. "How about offering your condolences?"

Her chest tightened, squeezing her lungs until she

found it difficult to breathe. His dark brown eyes ensnared her. She wanted to look away, but couldn't. She had never seen such fury or pain. It wouldn't take much to unleash it. If she moved he would pounce.

"I only just heard about Giovanni's car accident. I'm sorry for your loss."

Antonio's eyes narrowed and she could swear his anger quivered in the air.

"Such a display of grief for an ex-lover," he said in a raspy low tone. "It must have been a nasty break-up. What happened? Cheated on him, too?"

He didn't know. She breathed a little easier. "I did not have an affair with Giovanni," she said, holding her notepad and pen against her chest as if they could shield her from Antonio's wrath. She took a cautious step back.

"Bella, one more move…"

"*Signorina*," the man from the other table interrupted, "you forgot the—"

"One moment," Bella pleaded to the customer as she took the opportunity to shuffle away from Antonio. "I'll be right back."

She tried to march into the kitchen just as she felt Antonio's large hand fall on her shoulder. She still recognized his touch, she thought as she squeezed her eyes shut, fighting off the self-recrimination and longing swirling inside her.

Antonio whirled her around until she faced him. If he hadn't been holding her so tight she'd have collapsed. She felt so sick. So tired. Of worrying. Of barely surviving.

Isabella tilted her head back to look him in the eye. She had forgotten how powerfully tall he was. His height and strength had used to make her feel safe and protected. Now it made her feel extremely vulnerable.

"I've been looking for you," Antonio said. His voice was soft and dangerous. He lowered his head until he blocked out the rest of the world. "You were surprisingly difficult to find."

Isabella's stomach twisted with fear. Antonio placed both hands on her shoulders, his fingers digging into her like talons. He surrounded her. She felt caged. Trapped.

"What's going on here?" Her boss's harsh voice sounded close. "Isabella, what have you done?"

"I'll take care of it," she promised the older man without taking her eyes off Antonio. One touch, one look and she was his. It had always been that way.

The world started to spin and she swallowed roughly. She was mentally and physically exhausted. She wasn't at the top of her game when she needed to be the most. Why did Antonio have to reappear in her life when she was so fragile?

"I don't know why you bothered." Isabella took a quick glimpse and saw her boss next to the stove, saw his undisguised interest in the rich customer in his café. "You still think I was having an affair with Giovanni when I was with you."

Antonio's eyes darkened and his harsh features tightened with anger. "Oh, I *know* you were."

He hadn't forgiven his brother. Or her. He never would. Isabella swallowed hard, tapping into the last of her strength. She felt wobbly and weak, but the fight hadn't quite left her.

She just wished Antonio would take his hands off her. Her skin stung with awareness as tension whipped between them like a lash. She couldn't think straight when he touched her. She'd never been able to.

"I know you were his mistress," he drawled softly. "Why else would he leave you something in his will?"

Isabella cringed. That couldn't be good. She had thought Giovanni was her friend, letting her stay with him and helping her out. He hadn't revealed his true nature until it was too late. "Go away, Antonio. You don't know anything."

"I'm not leaving without you. You have to sign some documents in the law office as soon as possible."

Panic bloomed inside her. She wasn't going anywhere with Antonio. Isabella tried to show no expression, but she knew she'd failed when she saw the glint of dark satisfaction in Antonio's eyes. He wanted to make her uncomfortable. He wanted to see her suffer.

"Tell your family that you couldn't find me." She took a step away from Antonio and was relieved when he let go. "Give the money away to charity."

Antonio eyed her with disbelief. "You don't know how much it is."

"It doesn't matter." She could use the money, but she didn't trust this gift from Giovanni. There would be a price to pay if she accepted.

"Isabella!" her boss yelled. "Get the food on the table before it gets cold."

She turned abruptly and her head spun. She reached for the wall but her fingers gripped Antonio's strong arm. She battled desperately for her balance. She couldn't show weakness—or any other symptoms. She sensed Antonio's stare and held back a groan.

"You're ill?" he asked sharply.

"I didn't get much sleep last night," she replied in a rough voice.

She refused to look at him, not wanting him to see just how weak she truly felt. She could tell that he was assessing her and that made her worry. Antonio was smart and he'd made a fortune on intuitive connections. It wouldn't take him much longer to figure out what was wrong with her. She had to get away before he discovered the truth.

"Isabella!" her boss barked out.

"Let me serve this," Isabella told Antonio as she grabbed the tray of food. "Then we won't be interrupted again."

She didn't wait for his answer as she hurried out to the sidewalk. She served the food quickly, almost spilling it. She recovered just in time, murmuring her profuse apologies, but her mind was on possible escape routes. Isabella moved slightly until she was in a blind spot from the kitchen. This was her last chance to make a run for it.

Isabella placed the serving tray on one of the empty tables. She kept her casual pace until she turned the corner. Then she ran as fast as she could down the alley to the back stairs.

As her feet slapped against the pavement her lungs felt like they were going to explode—but she couldn't stop. Time was of the essence. Isabella reached the stairs and climbed them, two steps at a time. She tripped and bruised her knee. For a moment her world tilted, but she got back up and kept going.

Her legs burned and shook, but she pushed herself to go faster. Antonio would now have realized that she'd escaped. Any minute he'd start looking for her.

She reached the door to her room, but didn't stop to take a breath. She felt nauseous and her body ached. It didn't matter. She needed to get far away and then she would rest.

Swinging the door open, Isabella saw her backpack on the top of her lumpy mattress. She stepped into the small room and lunged for it. As she grasped the shoulder strap she heard the door bang shut.

Isabella turned around and the room moved. She saw Antonio resting against the door. He didn't look surprised or out of breath. From the glimmering rage in his dark eyes, she thought he had probably been waiting there for her the moment she stepped out of the kitchen.

"I'm disappointed, Bella," he said in a dangerously soft tone. "You're becoming so predictable."

"I—I…" She blinked as dark spots gathered along the edges of her eyes. She felt light-headed, but her arms and legs were unusually heavy. She couldn't move.

He stepped away from the door and approached her. "I don't have time for your games. You're coming with me *now*."

"I…" She needed to move. Run. Shamelessly lie.

But just as Antonio reached for her her head lolled back and she fainted, collapsing at his feet.

CHAPTER TWO

"BELLA!" Antonio sprung into action and caught her as her backpack fell onto the wooden floor with a thud. He lifted her and couldn't help noticing how light and delicate she was. *Fragile.* The word whispered in his mind like a warning.

She slumped against his arm and he held on tight as alarm pulsed through his veins. He swept the wisps of hair from her face. Her eyes were closed and her complexion was very pale. He laid her carefully on the mattress. Crouching down next to her, Antonio took a quick survey of the tiny room. The beige paint was peeling off the walls in chunks and a faint scent of rotting garbage wafted through the small open window. There was nothing else. No sink or refrigerator so he could get her water. There was hardly enough space for the mattress. How could she live like this? Why was she living here when she had a life and a future in America?

"Bella?" He tapped her cheek with his fingers. Her skin was soft and cold.

Isabella frowned and pursed her lips. She murmured something but it was incomprehensible. She didn't open her eyes.

Antonio started to get suspicious. His first instinct

had been to take care of Isabella. *Some things never change,* he thought bitterly. But what if this was an act? Did she hope that he would back off? Not a chance.

"Isabella," he called out sharply.

"Go away," she said drowsily. She turned to her side and curled her legs close to her chest.

"No." He grabbed her shoulder and gave her a shake.

"I'm serious." She squeezed her eyes shut and weakly tried to push his hand away. "Leave me alone."

He wished he could. He wished he had left her alone when he'd first seen her. It had been early March. The sun had been shining but there had been a chill in the air as he'd left his office. He had just pocketed his cell phone when he'd seen a young woman standing a few feet away on the sidewalk.

Antonio had done a double-take and halted.

"Is everything all right, sir?" his assistant had asked.

No. His world had taken a sudden tilt as he'd stared at the blonde, dressed simply in a fitted leather jacket, skintight jeans and knee-high boots. The violent kick of attraction had made him take a staggering step back.

He knew many beautiful young women, but there had been something different about this one. He had wanted to accept her silent challenge. It could have been her don't-mess-with-me stance or the jaunty tilt of her black fedora. Maybe it had been the bright red scarf draped around her neck that hinted at attitude. What-ever it was, he had found it irresistible.

"Sir?" his assistant had prompted.

Antonio had barely heard him. His attention had been on the blonde as she'd turned a map upside down, clearly hopeless at navigating. Then suddenly she'd shrugged her shoulders and stuffed the map carelessly into her backpack. Antonio had watched as the blonde had started walking away as if she was ready for whatever adventure she faced.

Her beauty and vitality had intrigued him, and her bold spirit had captured his imagination. He'd known he had to meet this woman or regret missing the opportunity.

"Cancel my meeting," he had said to his stunned assistant.

Following an elemental instinct he had not wanted to question, Antonio had ignored the chauffeured car waiting for him and followed the blonde.

His pulse had quickened as he'd watched the swing of her long blonde hair and the sway of her hips. She'd looked over her shoulder, and as their gazes connected he had seen the flare of attraction in her blue eyes. Instead of looking away she had turned and approached him.

"*Mi scusi*," she had said, her voice strong and clear as she'd met his gaze boldly. "Do you speak English?"

"Of course," he had said, noticing she was American. There had been no light of recognition in her eyes—just lust. She'd had no idea who he was.

"Great. I'm looking for the Piazza del Popolo," she had said, her attention clearly drawn to his mouth. She had absently swiped the tip of her tongue along her bottom lip.

Antonio had clenched his jaw. He had wanted to know how her lips tasted, but it had been too soon, too fast. The last thing he'd wanted to do was scare her off. "It's not far," he had replied gruffly as attraction pulsed between them. "I can show you where it is."

He had been fascinated as he'd watched her cheeks

turn pink. She hadn't tried to hide her interest, but she'd been fighting an internal struggle. He had seen the rise and fall of her chest and the eagerness in her expression. She had been tempted to explore whatever was happening between them.

"Wouldn't it be out of your way?"

"Not at all," he had lied. His voice had softened as his chest had tightened with growing excitement. "I happen to be going in that direction."

"What luck!" Her broad smile had indicated that she didn't believe him. She could have said she was going to Venice and he would have given the same answer. "By the way, I'm Isabella."

He had taken Bella to bed that night. There had been no games, no pretense. There had also been no indication that this American student on Spring Break would twist him in so many knots that he would never be the same again. She hadn't been very experienced, but a generous and affectionate lover.

Giovanni had thought so, too.

The reminder burned like acid, eating away at him.

Antonio stood up and shoved his clenched fists in his pockets. "You told me you weren't sick."

"I'm not sick," she countered faintly.

The Isabella he knew was full of life and ready to take on the world. This Isabella looked like a strong gust of wind would knock her over. "You need to see a doctor."

Isabella suddenly opened her eyes wide. She blinked a few times and darted a quick look at him before keeping her gaze on the floor. She rose, resting awkwardly on her elbow and pushing the wayward hair out of her face. "I've seen a doctor. I'm not sick. Just exhausted. All I need is to eat and sleep properly."

Antonio cast her a look of disbelief. "I would ask for a second opinion."

"I don't need one. Now, go away," she ordered with the flutter of her hand.

"I'm not leaving here without you."

"You have to," she urged as she held her head in her hands. "Tell everyone that you couldn't find me. Tell them that I'm back home."

It was tempting. He wanted to leave and not look back. Purge her from his memories. Do anything that would erase Isabella from his world. But he knew that was impossible.

"Sorry. I'm not like you. I choose to tell the truth whenever possible."

She lifted her head to glare at him. "I never lied to you. I never—"

He turned away and checked his watch. "I don't have time to rehash the past."

"Rehash?" Isabella's voice rose angrily. "When did we discuss it the first time around? I thought we were happy. We had been together for weeks and going strong. We had made love throughout the night. The next morning your security woke me up to kick me out. My bag was packed and you wouldn't take my call. You didn't tell me why you did that, and you never gave me a chance to talk about it!"

Antonio leaned against the wall by the door. The room felt like it was getting smaller. "I wasn't in the mood to hear your excuses. I'm even less inclined to now."

"There was nothing to excuse," Isabella argued as she rose slowly.

Her movements were wobbly and awkward. Antonio folded his arms so he wouldn't reach out and help her. He already regretted holding her close. He didn't like how much effort it had taken to pull away. His fingertips still stung from where he had touched her face.

Isabella looked him in the eye and jutted out her chin. "I did not have an affair."

He held up his hand. "Enough! I will not discuss it."

"Typical," she said with a sigh. "You don't like to discuss anything. Especially if it's personal. No matter how hard I tried, you wouldn't share how you felt. The only time I knew exactly what you were thinking was when we were in bed."

An intimate and very inconvenient image bloomed in his mind. Of Isabella, naked in his bed, eagerly following his explicit demands. When they'd been alone together he had held nothing back. He had demonstrated how much he wanted Isabella and how much her touch had meant to him. There had been many times when it hadn't been certain who was in command.

A muscle bunched in his jaw and ferocious energy swirled around him. "We are leaving," he announced in a gravelly tone. Antonio thrust the door open and waited for Isabella.

"No," she said firmly. "I'm not signing any papers. I don't want Giovanni's money."

"I'm sure you earned it." He didn't want her to know what was at stake here. All he wanted was to end this errand as soon as possible. By whatever means necessary. Antonio walked over to her.

Isabella's eyes widened. "Don't you dare touch me!"

"How times have changed," he said silkily as he wrapped his hand around her wrist. He ignored her racing pulse under his fingers as he picked up her backpack. "I remember when you begged for my touch."

Isabella tried futilely to pull out of his grasp. "I thought you didn't want to talk about the past? Let go of me."

"I will when we get to my car." If it was still where he had parked it. Trust Bella to find the most dangerous neighborhood to live in.

"I'm not going anywhere with you!" Isabella declared as she tried to grab onto the doorframe—but she couldn't hold on.

"Think again." He headed for the stairs, dragging her behind him.

"Pushy and selfish," she muttered. "It must be a Rossi trait. You are just like your brother."

Antonio stilled as the accusation lashed at him. He slowly turned and faced Isabella. He saw the wariness in her eyes as she backed away. She didn't get far as his grip tightened around her wrist. "*Don't.*"

Isabella's gaze fell to her feet. "All I meant—"

"I don't care what you meant." Her words had clawed open a wound he had valiantly tried to ignore. Were he and Gio interchangeable in Isabella's mind? How often had she thought of his brother when she'd kissed *him*? Had she responded the same way in Gio's bed?

His thoughts turned darker, piercing his soul. Antonio didn't say anything as he took a step closer to Isabella, backing her against the wall. Why had she chosen Gio over him? Everyone else he knew made that choice, but why Isabella? He had thought she was different. Was it because Gio had been the handsome and charismatic one? Had his brother fulfilled her deepest, darkest fantasies? Or had she actually fallen in love with his brother?

"Antonio?" she whispered with uncertainty.

He stared at Isabella. Her angelic beauty hid a devious nature. Her bold spirit and breathtaking innocence had led him straight to a hell that he might never escape. He blinked slowly as he battled the darkness enveloping him. He wouldn't let this woman destroy him again.

Antonio released her wrist as if her touch burned. He took a deliberate step back but met her eyes with a steady gaze. "Don't compare me with my brother. *Ever.*"

Isabella couldn't move as she stared into his brown eyes. Her heart twisted and her breath snagged in her throat. Antonio was always so careful not to show his thoughts and emotions, but now they were laid bare before her. The man was in torment.

But just as quickly as he'd exposed his pain his eyes were shuttered. When he opened them again he was back in control, while *her* emotions were in a jumbled mess.

Antonio turned away from her and Isabella sagged against the wall. She slowly exhaled as her heart pounded in her ears. She felt shaky, her limbs twitching as she watched Antonio take the stairs.

"I'm sorry."

Her words were just a whisper but she saw Antonio's rigid stance as he silently deflected her apology.

She hadn't meant to compare Antonio to his brother. They had very different personalities. It was impossible to confuse the two. Giovanni had been a charmer, with movie star looks, always the life of the party. He'd been entertaining—but not fascinating like Antonio.

The moment she had met Antonio she'd known he was out of her league. She didn't have the sophistication or sexual knowledge to hold on to him. It hadn't mattered. She'd only wanted to be with him. Just once.

Isabella remembered when they had first met and he had offered to show her Piazza del Popolo. The sight of him had jolted her as if she had woken from a deep slumber. Her heart had started to race when she saw him.

She knew she had projected an image of being bold and strong. Tough. It had all been an act. It had been her way of protecting herself as she went through the world alone. But the way the man had been looking at her—she had felt brazen. She had wanted to hold on to that feeling.

"I'm Antonio," he had said, and offered his hand.

She had hesitated at the sight of his expensive cuff-links. It had only been then that she'd noticed he wore a designer suit. His silk tie had probably cost more than her round-trip ticket to Italy. She didn't know anyone who had that kind of money.

Be careful of the rich ones. Her mother words had drifted in her head. *They only want one thing from women like us.*

Isabella had smiled. She had decided that it was okay because she was after the same thing.

She had reached for Antonio's hand and felt a sharp tingle as her skin had glided against his. She hadn't been able to hide her gasp of surprise. When she had tried to pull away Antonio had wrapped his long, strong fingers around her hand.

Instead of making her feel trapped, his touch had pierced through the gray numbness that had settled in her when she had nursed her mother through her final illness. Her breath had locked in her throat as he'd raised her hand to his mouth.

The earthy colors of Rome had deepened and the sun had turned golden. The blaring sound of traffic had faded as Antonio had brushed his lips against her knuckles. She had known that this man would be the highlight of her vacation. She hadn't expected to fall in love—and into his bed—with such wild abandon.

She hadn't expected that she would never be the same again.

Isabella jerked her mind to the present as she saw Antonio disappear from the stairwell with her backpack. Everything she owned—her passport, her money—was in there.

"Wait!" she called out, and hurriedly followed him. She rounded the building and saw Antonio striding down the block. Isabella ran after him. "Antonio, stop!"

He walked to his sports car—a menacing-looking machine that was as black as night. He punched a button on his keyring and the small trunk popped open. Isabella watched in horror as he tossed her backpack in and slammed it shut.

"Give me back my bag," she said as she reached the car.

"You'll get it after we visit the lawyers."

"You don't understand, Antonio. I have to work." She gestured at the café on the other end of the block.

"Who cares?" He walked to the driver's side. "This is more important."

Spoken like a man who had never had to scrape by

or go hungry. "I'm already going to get in trouble for taking an unscheduled break."

"Unscheduled break? You made a run for it and you weren't planning to return."

"I can't afford to lose this job." She rubbed her hand over her forehead as she tried to maintain her composure. "If I get fired I lose my room."

He glanced up at the broken rusted window of her room. "It won't be that big of a loss."

Isabella put her hands on her hips. "Maybe not to you, but this job is the only thing that is keeping me from becoming homeless!"

Antonio's eyes narrowed. "Is this about money?"

"What?" She stared at him across the car.

"Of course it is."

"It's about my *livelihood*," she corrected him through clenched teeth. Antonio wouldn't understand about that, having been born into wealth and status. She needed her job because she had no other form of support or resources. Why couldn't he see that? "Listen, let's make a compromise. I will go to the lawyers with you once I finish my shift at the café."

Antonio took another look at his watch. "That's unacceptable."

"Seriously? How is that unacceptable? You asked for a favor from me and I just agreed to do it."

"We both know you are prolonging the inevitable and will try to avoid it. Although I find it very curious that you aren't asking how much money you will get. Unless, of course, you already know."

"There's nothing curious about it," she said as she folded her arms protectively around her. "The only thing I know is that any money will come with strings attached. I don't want anything—especially if it means dealing with you or your family."

Antonio chose to ignore her comment. "I'm not willing to wait around and watch over you until your shift ends."

"Do you even know how to compromise?" she asked, tossing her hands up in frustration. Of course he didn't. The world bowed down to him. Just as she had done, once upon a time.

"This is what I know," he said as he slipped on his sunglasses. "The will was read three days ago. The contents will soon become public."

Isabella frowned. "What are you talking about?"

He opened the door and sat down in the driver's seat. "It won't take long before the paparazzi find you."

She jerked her head back in surprise. "Paparazzi? What would they want with me?"

"You're kidding, right? The woman who slept with the Rossi brothers has wound up with a fortune."

She stared at him with wide eyes. "There is no need to make it sound so salacious."

"I'm just telling it like it is," he said impatiently. "Now, get in."

Isabella hesitated. Giovanni had left her a fortune? That couldn't be right. Antonio must be exaggerating. If only she *could* accept the money. But even if she did it would take ages to go through the legal and financial systems and get the cash she so desperately needed.

What would happen to her after she'd signed the documents? She had no home, no money and no protection. She had been working for months to raise the money to get back to California and she didn't think she would make enough before the paparazzi found her. Could she ask Antonio for help?

She bit her lip as she weighed the pros and cons. *Could* she ask him? Was she willing to stoop that low? Antonio could easily afford the price of a plane ticket, probably had the cash in his wallet, but it felt wrong.

Antonio leaned back in his seat. "What do you want?"

She took a deep breath. "I need a plane ticket to Los Angeles. For tonight."

He nodded sharply. "What else?"

She was already regretting her request. She didn't want anything from Antonio. His presence reminded her of the poor choices she made because she'd been in love. She had fought for him, for them, and he had discarded her without a second thought. As much as it pained her to think about it, her mother had been right. She hated it when that happened.

"That's it."

He tipped his sunglasses and studied her face. "I don't believe you."

"That doesn't surprise me," she replied. "But I mean it. I don't want anything else."

"That will change soon," he said as he started the engine.

"Maybe I didn't make myself clear. I shall consider this a loan," she said as the car purred to life. "I'll pay you back once I get settled."

"It's not necessary."

"It is," she insisted. "It wouldn't be right to take your money."

"I don't care about the money." Antonio said. "Get in the car."

Isabella hesitated. Was that wise? The man hated her. He thought she'd betrayed him. Then again, he probably wanted her out of Italy and out of his life as soon as possible. She had nothing to worry about.

"Bella..." Antonio's tone warned of his growing impatience.

Isabella opened the door and sat down before she changed her mind. "Don't expect me to stay long," she said as she reached for the seatbelt. "I'll sign the papers and then I'm gone."

And if she were lucky she would never see Antonio again.

CHAPTER THREE

"This is a law office?" Isabella asked as she studied the old building. "I haven't seen one like this before."

Antonio glanced up and saw that the façade was pale, almost pink-gold. He noticed the faded mosaics next to the arched windows and pillars. It was strange that he'd never really looked at the building before.

"Where did you think I would take you?"

"You don't want me to answer that," she muttered.

They entered the dark and musty building. It was unnaturally quiet and the only sound was their footsteps as they climbed the stairs. The silence Antonio shared with Isabella felt strange but he was grateful for it. He didn't need to think about the easy conversations they'd once had that would last throughout the night. He didn't want to remember how he'd used to call her up during the day just to hear her voice. He wanted the barrier of silence. Needed it.

The receptionist took one look at Isabella and sniffed with disapproval. Antonio glared at the dour woman, letting her know that he wouldn't tolerate that kind of behavior. The woman bent her head from the silent reprimand and icily escorted them to the conference room.

When the door opened Antonio saw his mother, sitting regally next to the ornate rosewood table. Dressed severely in black, Maria Rossi was as elegant and private as always. She was trying to hide her distress, but he instantly saw it in her face.

"Mother, why are you here?" Antonio asked. "Your presence isn't required."

His mother's expression darkened when she saw Isabella at her side. "Is this the woman?"

"This is Isabella Williams," Antonio said with a hint of warning.

He reluctantly introduced Isabella to his mother. He had hoped to prevent these two women from meeting. With one wintry glance Maria made it clear what she thought of Isabella. She knew this blonde beauty was the reason her sons had been estranged.

Antonio's first instinct was to protect Isabella from the slight. But that didn't make sense. She was in the wrong and should suffer the consequences. She had created a scandal when she'd started living with Giovanni. The paparazzi had gone into a feeding frenzy, and had Antonio borne the brunt of the gossip. But he still couldn't stand by and watch Isabella receive this treatment.

Most socialites he knew would have wilted under his mother's apparent disgust. To his surprise, Isabella tilted her head proudly. She wasn't going to back down or hang her head in shame. She stood before this doyenne of high society in her cheap clothes, with her tarnished name, and held her gaze unflinchingly.

His mother was the first to break eye contact. She

turned to him. "I can't bear to be in the same room with her."

Isabella showed no expression as she watched Maria Rossi leave the room and closed the door with a flourish.

"I apologize for my mother's behavior," Antonio said, fighting back anger. "I'll see that it doesn't happen again."

"No need," Isabella crossed her arms and walked to the large window. "I know you feel the same way."

Antonio watched her as she stared at the view of the Pantheon. He suspected she wasn't really looking at anything. It was as if she was in another time, another place, trapped in a memory.

If only he could do the same. His mind was always racing, predicting problems and creating solutions. He required an outlet for his inexhaustible energy and found it in his work. The money and power that came along with it wasn't important. Antonio needed the challenge, to push himself to the razor's edge.

There had been one time when he hadn't felt that drive, and that had been when he was with Isabella. When they'd been together nothing else had existed. Isabella Williams had been his escape. And eventually his downfall.

"What did you tell your mother about me?" Isabella grimaced as the question sprang from her lips. She hadn't meant to ask, but it was obvious that her reputation had preceded her. Isabella knew she shouldn't care but it bothered her.

There was something about Antonio's mother that intimidated her. The woman was beautifully groomed, from her coiffed hair to her pedicured feet, but she also had an aura of power. No one would treat Maria Rossi with anything less than respect. Isabella had felt grubby next to her.

"We never discussed you," he said stiffly.

She wouldn't be surprised if that were true. Antonio rarely discussed his family. Everything she knew about his mother and his late father had come from Giovanni. And he'd probably been just as private about his love life with his family.

Isabella turned and approached Antonio. "But she knows you and I were once together?"

"Not from me."

"Giovanni?" No wonder his mother hated her.

"My mother was prying into the reason why her sons weren't on speaking terms again." Antonio crossed his arms and looked away. "I'm sure Gio concocted some story that made him look like the innocent victim."

"Again?" Her tired brain caught onto that word. "You and Giovanni had been estranged before?"

Antonio's jaw clenched. "Yes."

She felt the weight of guilt lift a little. All this time she'd thought she had ruined the strong bond between brothers. "But how could that be?" she asked as she remembered Giovanni and Antonio together. They'd had a tendency to use the same expressions, finish each other's sentences. "You two were close."

Antonio shrugged. "Gio had been trying to make amends and was on his best behavior. It was one of the few times we got along."

"Why did you accept him back into your life?" That didn't seem like something Antonio would do. You screwed up once and you were banished from Antonio's life. You didn't get another chance.

"I thought he had changed." He sighed. "I wanted him to change."

She saw the grief in his expression. She wanted to reach out and bring him comfort, but she knew Antonio would not appreciate the gesture. "How old were you when you first stopped talking to each other?"

His harsh features tightened. "I don't want to discuss it."

"Why not?"

"I answered your questions, now it's my turn."

Isabella jerked her head back. She saw the intensity in his eyes, the determined set of his jaw. Was he really trying to deflect her questions or had this all been a technique to draw her closer? Make her think he was opening up to her so she would feel obligated to do the same?

Isabella braced her shoulders. "I didn't agree to that."

"Why did Gio include you in his will?"

"I have no idea. I didn't ask him to." But she suspected she knew the answer. Giovanni had been playing games and now she was going to lose everything.

"The lawyers say that Gio changed his will a month ago."

Isabella paled. That could not be a coincidence. "S-so?"

Antonio tilted his head to one side as he studied her face. "You know why. No one else does. No one knows why he gave you millions."

"M-millions?" she whispered. "That doesn't make any sense."

"And half the shares in Rossi Industries."

"What?" The shock reverberated through her body.

"He gave you half my birthright," Antonio said in a growl.

She clapped her hand over her mouth. *Oh, Giovanni. What have you done? Why did you do this?*

"I lost part of my birthright once before," his said, his voice a harsh whisper. "I have no intention of losing it again."

Isabella frowned. She felt like she was missing crucial information. "What are you talking about?"

Antonio didn't hear her. "Why did Gio give all this to *you*? Why not the woman he was dating? Why not a woman who meant something to him? Why *you*?"

"Antonio…" She braced her legs and held her clenched hands at her sides. She didn't have the nerve to tell him. She didn't want to face the consequences.

"Was it so I would be required to work with the woman who had cheated on me?"

Had Giovanni done this out of spite? For his own perverse pleasure? It was possible…

"Or did you seduce it out of him? I admit you're good in bed—but *that* good?"

Isabella felt the heat in her cheeks. If only she could run away. The moment she uttered the next words everything would change. Everything would be lost.

"It's because I'm p-pregnant."

He stared at her in shock. Isabella hunched her shoulders, preparing for the world to fall around her as struggled to get the words out.

She nervously licked her lips before she added, "And Giovanni *is* the father."

Antonio staggered back as if he had been punched. His body went numb and his mind whirled. His world tilted and he swayed. He wanted to grab hold of something so he wasn't brought to his knees, but that meant reaching out to Isabella. The one woman who still had the power to hurt him.

"You…"

Isabella was having his brother's baby. Gio had known and hadn't told him. The pain radiated through his body.

"But I didn't have an affair with him. I swear."

An affair. A fling. Sex. It was all the same.

Antonio held up his hand. Rage billowed through him, crimson, hot and bitter. "You're pregnant," he said, as if he was in a daze. "How many months?"

She held her hands in front of her stomach. "I'm just past the first trimester."

"Three months?" he muttered as the fury seized his throat.

"Antonio, you have to believe me," she pleaded. "I only slept with him one time."

He fought back the red mist that threatened to overtake him. "*Only?* Is a one-night stand supposed to make me feel better?" he asked in a low, biting tone. Was he supposed to believe that when she had lived with Giovanni for *weeks*?

Isabella's face tightened with anger. "How many women have you slept with since we broke up?"

"That's not the issue. Those women were not the *reason* we broke up." He would not allow Isabella to distract him. "I kicked you out because you were sleeping with my brother. Now you're telling me you're carrying his child."

"It happened the night I heard on the news that you

were going to marry someone else." Isabella spoke halt-
ingly, as if the memory still tormented her.

"And that's your excuse?" He stared at her. He didn't
know if she was feeding him lies or if she was planning
to thrust another knife in his back.

"No. I'm trying to explain." She covered her face
with her hands. "I was emotional and I drank far too
much. I had been like that for weeks. I was self-destruc-
tive and I made a lot of poor choices during that time.
I'm not proud of what I did."

But she had done it. Would she have told him about
Giovanni if she wasn't pregnant, or would she have
taken her secret to the grave?

"Do you wind up in the nearest bed whenever you
drink?"

She slowly lowered her hands. "I'm not sure what
happened that night."

"How convenient."

She glared at him. "All I know is that I was an emotional mess. You had kicked me out, you didn't want to
have anything to do with me, and then I heard you were
planning a future with another woman."

"And what better way to get back at me than by
sleeping with my brother?" He'd used to think Isabella
was sweet and innocent, but she had hidden a venge-
ful streak. The people closest to him had warned him
about Isabella, but he hadn't listened. He'd thought he
knew everything about her. But it turned out he didn't
know her at all.

"I didn't know about your history with Giovanni."
Isabella stood rigid in front of him, her clenched fists
at her sides. "I didn't know you had discarded me like

a piece of trash because you thought I'd had an affair with your brother."

"And look at what you did," Antonio said. The red mist was creeping in and he was feeling dangerous. Out of control like never before. Antonio shoved his shaky hands in his pockets.

"Giovanni planned this!" she blurted out. "He took advantage of me."

"I'm sure he got you into bed in record time." Bile rose from his stomach and he wanted to be violently ill.

She thrust out her chin. "I'm not like that," she said in a trembling voice.

"Yes, you are," he said with a sneer. "You were with *me*."

Isabella eyes widened as if she'd been hit. "You throw that back in my face?" she asked in a shocked whisper. "What we had was different. It was special. It was—"

"Part of your routine," he finished coldly. "Only Gio got you pregnant. Was that planned or an unexpected bonus? Is that why he kicked you out?"

"He didn't kick me out. I left the next morning," she told him, her voice wobbling with emotion. "I didn't feel safe there anymore. I ran as fast as I could."

Antonio frowned and he crossed his arms. Her explanation niggled at him. Something didn't add up. "Then how did he know about the baby?"

"I told him when I found out. That was a month ago."

And his brother had changed his will a month ago. "What did Gio say?"

"Not much." Isabella looked away abruptly.

"Isabella," he warned in a firm tone, "tell me."

Her shoulders sagged in defeat and her expression

turned grim. "He laughed," she answered. "He said, 'Antonio will never touch you now!' and he laughed like a madman."

Antonio took a step back. He shouldn't be surprised, but he was. He hadn't fully appreciated the depth of his brother's hatred.

"And he was right." She gestured at him, the simple movement indicating her disappointment. "He knew exactly how you'd react if you found out the truth."

"That's why you ran away at the café?" Isabella had been afraid of how he would react. And she was smart, because right now he wanted to lash out. He wanted to smash and destroy everything around him. "You are not the woman I thought you were."

"That's not true," she spat angrily. "You just want to hear bad things about me. It's easier for you because you're looking for my faults."

Easier? He felt like he had been ripped apart. He was never going to be the same again.

She gulped in a ragged breath. "I want you to know that I didn't cheat on you."

"How can I know that? How can I believe you weren't sleeping with my brother from the first day you met him?"

"I have no way of proving it. Why can't you—?"

A polite knock on the double doors interrupted them. Isabella jumped back and pressed her lips together as a withered old man with snowy white hair in a black three-piece suit entered the room.

Antonio tried to rein in his emotions as he tersely introduced the lawyer to Isabella. The older man invited her into his office and she silently followed. As she passed Antonio he grabbed Isabella's wrist, forcing her to stop.

"This discussion isn't over," he said.

"Yes, it is," she said coldly as she pulled away from his grasp. "I don't have to explain myself to you. You have no rights over me *or* my child."

Isabella walked through the door and the lawyer followed. Antonio stared at the closed door, his body rigid as an idea formed.

"Not yet," Antonio murmured. "But I once I do there will be hell to pay."

CHAPTER FOUR

"I'M GOING to be a grandmother." Maria Rossi sighed and clasped her hands together. "Gio's child. Oh, I hope it will look just like him."

"I'm glad to see you're taking this well," Antonio muttered as he'd paced the floor of the conference room. He should have left his mother in the waiting room but he had to tell her that their situation had changed. Their strategy had been blown apart by Isabella's bombshell.

"I admit Gio had no business putting her in the will." His mother's voice was thick with annoyance. "Giving money and power to *that* woman."

"He did it to cut me out."

"No, Gio wouldn't do that to you. He wouldn't," she insisted as he made a face. "That woman bewitched him. He wasn't thinking straight. I can understand making provision for the child—but all that money?" Maria shuddered delicately. "We don't know if it's even his."

"We'll find out." But Antonio's instincts told him that the baby *was* Gio's. His brother wouldn't have pulled this stunt unless he had been absolutely sure. Gio wanted his child to inherit and gave Isabella the power over the money and shares until the child comes of age.

"Gio told me himself that that Jezebel seduced

him," his mother continued. "You both should have known better. I don't know what either of you saw in the woman."

He could easily make a list of things he had seen in Isabella, but it would scandalize his mother. Antonio raked his hand through his hair. "I don't want to hear it."

"There's only one way a girl like her can land a rich man. She has to get pregnant."

Antonio slammed his hand against the mahogany table so hard that Maria jumped. "That's enough." It also wasn't true. Isabella had had *him* wrapped around her little finger without an unplanned pregnancy.

"Temper, temper," Maria said as she patted her chignon. "If you plan to get full control of the Rossi fortune you need to show some patience."

Antonio walked to the window and leaned against the pane. "I have one or two plans," he admitted. He wasn't happy about either of them. Both required him to get very close to the woman who betrayed him.

"How many months along is she?"

He had been reluctant to ask for details, but at the same time his mind was filled with questions. "She says she's at least three months pregnant. I kicked her out the last week of May, so I know the baby isn't mine. She left Gio on the first of July and that fits the timeframe."

"You need to do something."

"I know. It leaves me two options. I can seduce her into giving up her inheritance and leaving the country for good."

But history had proved that he didn't have an infinite amount of sexual power over her. Isabella had left his bed to go into Gio's. He wasn't sure if he could seduce Isabella knowing she was carrying his brother's child.

"No," his mother said firmly. "That child is the only thing I have left of Gio. I want it to be part of my life."

Antonio inhaled sharply as jagged pain burned through him. His mother had had no problem banning *him* from her life when he had needed her the most. But then she'd still had Gio around.

"What is the second option?" she asked.

"Marry her and adopt the child as my own. That way I would have full control over the Rossi fortune."

He had never thought about becoming a father. As the second son, he'd felt no pressure to sire an heir. Now he might be required to accept Gio's child as his own. That baby would be a constant reminder of betrayal.

"That would be perfect," his mother said. "We wouldn't have to give up anything."

Just his freedom, Antonio thought he looked out of the window and gazed at the Pantheon. *And his peace of mind*. If there had been any other way he wouldn't have gone looking for Isabella. Now he might have to bind himself to the cheating vixen for the rest of his life.

"I really don't think this is a good idea," Isabella said as she entered Antonio's penthouse apartment. She heard the door close behind her and flinched when she heard it lock.

"I agree," Antonio said, "but the paparazzi have already found out about your windfall and my home is the safest place. Anyway, it's only for one night."

Isabella scoffed. As if that meant anything. She had slept with Antonio within hours of meeting him. But she wasn't going to tumble into his bed again, she reminded herself. He didn't want her anymore. He had someone else in his life.

But, to her shame, she knew that fact wouldn't stop her from falling into his arms. Despite everything—despite the way he'd discarded her and cast her out of his life—she still longed for Antonio's touch.

Isabella rubbed her bare arms as she stepped into the drawing room. She looked around and noticed that not much had changed. In fact the only thing different about the apartment was her. She was no longer the carefree and impetuous girl who'd seen the beauty in this room but not the power behind it. Back then she had put her dreams on hold for the man she loved. These days she had to play it safe. She would hold back instead of brazenly going forward. She had to protect herself and her baby's future.

She frowned when she noticed how quiet the apartment was. No music. No easy conversation. No laughter. The room was modern and dramatic. The sleek contemporary furniture and bold artwork were at odds with the panoramic view of Rome's ancient ruins. Isabella had always thought the apartment suited Antonio, a self-made man who bridged innovation and tradition. He'd conquered the business world with cutthroat strategy, but there was a dark sensuality about him that he contained ruthlessly. Yet *she* had seen it. In the artwork he was drawn to, in his movement, in his eyes.

She knew Antonio wanted a showdown, and he had brought her here because he wanted it on his territory. This place held wild memories. Did he think it would distract her? Or would he use their past as a way to seduce the truth out of her?

"The housekeeper has made up the guestroom for you," he said as he walked across the room.

"Thank you." She wished the housekeeper were here.

She didn't want to be alone with Antonio. She didn't trust him. She didn't trust herself.

She watched him as he strode to a table that held drinks. She tried to look away, but she couldn't. His striking features were so harsh and aggressive. Her hands tingled as she remembered brushing her fingertips along his slanted cheekbones and angular jaw. He radiated masculine power and raw sensuality. He had discarded the suit jacket that had cloaked his lean, muscular build. She dragged her gaze away so she wouldn't stare at his broad shoulders or sculpted chest.

"Would you like a drink?" he asked as he grabbed a decanter from the table. He froze and stared at the crystal in his hands. "I forgot. You can't drink alcohol."

"It's not just because I'm pregnant." She returned her attention to the window and looked out onto the night sky. "I don't drink anymore."

She heard Antonio pause in pouring a glass of whiskey. "Why is that?"

When she had stayed with Giovanni she had gotten caught up in his party circuit. She'd drunk to dull the pain. To forget. She hadn't realized she was out of control until she woke up in Giovanni's bed. "I overindulged one night and swore I wouldn't drink again."

"That often happened when you socialized with Gio and his friends."

"Yes, I found that out." She couldn't hide the bitterness in her voice.

"You couldn't keep up with his wild ways?" he asked as he took a sip of his drink.

Isabella breathed deeply and leaned against the cold glass. She had to control her temper. Had to keep her wits about her. She knew Antonio was going to interrogate her. "I thought you didn't want to talk about this?"

"I don't."

She believed that. He didn't want to know, but he had to find out. The curiosity was killing him. "Did you think for a minute that Giovanni might have lied to you?" Isabella asked. "That I might have been faithful to you?"

He stilled. "Yes," he said slowly.

The surprised her. Antonio didn't second-guess himself. "When was that?" she asked, watching him down his drink in one swallow.

"The day after you left." He curled his lip and set his glass down. "I considered the possibility that I made a mistake."

Isabella pulled away from the window. "And?"

"I made some enquiries." His expression darkened and he braced his hands on the table. "Only to discover that you had rolled out of my bed and into my brother's."

Isabella closed her eyes as she heard the raw pain in Antonio's voice. "It wasn't like that," she whispered.

"Right." His voice was low and biting as he glared at her. "You had already been in his bed before you left mine."

Isabella rubbed her forehead as tension pulsed underneath her skin. "I went to Giovanni because you had thrown me out. I had nowhere to go."

Antonio snorted with derision. "Hardly. You were right where you wanted to be."

She shook her head. "I wanted to be with you."

"Until you met my brother." Antonio walked over to where she stood. "You used your relationship with me so you could get closer to Gio and his money."

"I have never been interested in that!" Isabella said. She was surprised that he would think that of her, and she was also hurt that he didn't really know her at all.

"I thought I knew you." Antonio rested his arm against the window.

"You knew everything." But either he hadn't listened or he didn't care to remember. "Unlike you, I didn't hold anything back."

"Is this another stab at how I don't communicate?" He leaned forward, towering over her. "I disagree. We talked all the time."

She flattened her hand against her chest. "I did the talking. You didn't share anything. I didn't know about your hopes and fears. Your family life. You told me nothing."

"We're talking now," he said softly. "Tell me, how long were you sleeping with my brother when we were sharing a bed?"

"I was always satisfied in your bed. I didn't need to look elsewhere."

Isabella bit her lip, knowing she shouldn't have spoken so boldly. She saw the sensual heat flare in Antonio's eyes. Her skin tingled in response as a kaleidoscope of images swirled in her head. Tension curled around her. It was dangerous to bring up those memories. Isabella nervously cleared her throat.

"If that was true, why did you go to my brother in the first place?" he asked. "Why didn't you go back to California?"

Isabella sighed. She had asked herself that many times in the past three months. "I should have gone back home, but I thought we could get back together. I hoped it was a rough patch we could work through."

Antonio's eyes widened with disbelief. "Work through the fact that you were sleeping with my brother?"

"I didn't know you thought that I had!" she said in a raised voice. "How could I? You didn't share your suspicions with anyone. I didn't know anything. I only found out about Giovanni's lies three months ago."

Antonio's eyes narrowed as he watched Isabella's face. Impatience scratched at him. "Why did you think I dumped you?" he asked as he tugged his silk tie loose.

"I thought you had found someone else. When your security kicked me out, I tried to get in touch with you," she said coolly. Her eyes were blank, her composure restored. "You were blocking my calls. I went to your office and couldn't even get through the door."

He had cut her out of his life ruthlessly. He wouldn't deny that. It had been the only way he could get through the day. The nights had been the worst. He hadn't thought a man could crave a woman so strongly until Isabella had gone out of his life.

Isabella shrugged. "So I called Giovanni."

"You had his number?" Antonio gritted his teeth. He knew he was being possessive, but he didn't like the idea of Isabella having had *any* man's phone number.

"I told him what had happened and he invited me to his place." Isabella looked down and whispered, "I thought he was my friend."

"You two got along very well whenever I was around."

"Giovanni got along with everyone. But I wasn't interested in him," she said. "The only thing we had in common was you. When we talked, it was always about you."

"Why does that send a chill down my spine?"

Her mouth tightened into a straight line as she struggled with her temper. "I didn't know what your relationship was like. And when I accepted his invitation to stay I thought it would only be a day or two before you came to your senses. I kept trying to contact you but you blocked me in every way."

If she hadn't been living with his brother he would have crawled back and grovelled. But she had shown her true colors too early.

"Then, about the third day I stayed at Giovanni's, he told me that you had cut him out of his life because he'd taken sides."

"I cut him out of my life because he slept with *you*."

"Like I said," she bit out through clenched teeth, "I had no idea you thought that. I felt incredibly guilty for causing a rift between two brothers."

"Which you decided to fix by staying with him?" he asked, poking holes in her story. "How would that repair anything?"

"Giovanni told me it would all blow over and I believed him." She shook her head at her obvious mistake. "And, like a fool, I kept trying to contact you. He convinced me that I wasn't going to get you back by crying myself to sleep every night. He suggested I go out, act like I was having a good time, and remind you of what you were missing."

She'd done that very well. It had been difficult for him, coming back to this apartment every evening and knowing she wouldn't be there. Knowing she was in another man's bed. "You went out with Gio every night."

She nodded and slumped against the window.

"There were pictures of you and Gio in the papers. Every day." She had looked happy, relaxed and very sexy.

"I wasn't trying to make you jealous," she insisted. "Since I couldn't see or talk to you, it was my way of reminding you that I was still around."

"Clinging to his arm?" he added sharply.

Isabella scowled at him. "I did no such thing."

Antonio remembered how she'd used to cling to *him*. She'd curled up against him whether they were walking along the street, sitting on the sofa, or making love. It had been as though she couldn't get close enough. And he had welcomed the warmth and affection.

"In those tiny dresses."

Isabella blushed. She looked away and turned until her back pressed against the window. "That was probably a bad idea."

"Dresses that Gio bought you." They had been short, tight and revealing. The kind of dresses a man gave his mistress. "When you wouldn't accept any gift from me."

"I didn't have anything acceptable to wear to those events," she mumbled as she flattened her hands against the glass pane.

"And I didn't take you anywhere but to bed?"

She looked up sharply. "That's not true! We had so much fun exploring the city. I got to see Rome through your eyes."

"Obviously that wasn't enough." *He* wasn't enough, no matter what he had done and what he had given. "But you made up for lost time by attending every nightclub."

"I wasn't interested in those parties. Or those people. I preferred the places we went to alone."

He'd like to believe that. When he had learned she

was an art history student he had gone out of his way to take her to see private art collections and participate in specially guided tours. He had ignored all invitations to dinner parties and exclusive events because he hadn't wanted to share Isabella.

He'd thought she had felt the same. Isabella had never complained, or asked to go dancing. Isabella had never felt a need to dress up or entertain. The only other person who'd spent any time with them was his brother.

"If any of this is true, what made you leave Gio?"

She pressed her lips together. "I discovered that Giovanni was not my friend. He pounced when I was at my most vulnerable."

Antonio waited, but she didn't reveal any more details. "You'll have to do better than that."

Isabella exhaled slowly. "And then I found out about the lies he had spread. I was not unfaithful to you, and I don't know why you would have believed him. You should have confronted me," Isabella said, her voice wavering with emotion. "You should have told me about your suspicions."

He should have, but he knew what would have happened. He would have accepted her version because he'd wanted to believe her. He had wanted to be with her at any cost. Even now her story seemed plausible, even though she was carrying his brother's baby.

"But you cast me out." She gestured to the front door with a flutter of her hand. "You had your security staff do your dirty work. I would never have thought you'd take the coward's way out."

He had been cold and ruthless, but it had been an act of self-preservation. Isabella would have wrapped her magic around him, distracted him from the truth and made him believe anything.

Like she was doing now.

Right now he wanted to lean into Isabella. Sink into her soft, warm curves. Erase the past and drag her back to his bed. He was fighting her lure, but it was a losing battle. Her power over his senses, his mind, was humbling.

"How am I the coward?" he asked. "You ran away when you saw me."

"Why do you seem so surprised? I knew that seeing you again would destroy everything I've done so far to recover."

Her actions had caused her downfall, not his. "And that's why it's imperative that you return to America?" he asked. "Why do you need to leave immediately?"

"I want to go home and start over again." Her mournful voice pulled at him. "I want to forget Italy and everything that happened here."

Her words tore at him. Isabella had been the most important part of his life. Everything had fallen by the wayside when they were together. He had treated her like a queen and put her needs first, but it hadn't been enough for her.

Now she wanted to forget all that. She would move on while he stayed behind, haunted by memories wherever he went.

"I want to forget you."

He flinched as if he had been stabbed. No, he wouldn't let that happen. They'd shared heaven together and now they would share hell. He wasn't going to be the only one in torment. He would not carry the burden alone.

"I won't let you," he said. He stood in front of her, trapping her against the window. "I'm going to make you remember what we had and you will regret everything you did to destroy it."

CHAPTER FIVE

ANTONIO'S kiss was hot, hard and possessive. Isabella felt the kick of exhilaration before it rushed through her bloodstream. Her skin heated as she softened against him.

The flare in his dark eyes had been her only warning before his mouth claimed hers. At first she didn't fight it. She'd never thought she'd get the chance again, and his kiss was just as magical as she remembered.

Raw emotions crashed through her as she responded to his rough, hard mouth. He tasted of sensual, masculine power and a secret part of her wanted to surrender. Her heart pounded against her chest. Her flesh prickled with anticipation.

Isabella knew she needed to pull away. She had to stop this madness before she passed the point of no return. Had to break the spell. She had to find a way to keep her distance from Antonio.

Following her most primal instinct, Isabella sank her teeth into his bottom lip.

Antonio reared back. The red mark on his mouth should have made her feel guilty, but it gave her a dark satisfaction seeing her brand on him. She felt the angry puff of his breath and risked a look at his eyes.

An unholy glow leapt in them, and his face was taut with lust. Excitement lit through her body. She had unleashed something wickedly sensual she didn't think she could control.

Antonio crushed her against him, his strong arms caging her. She gasped as her breasts pressed hard against his chest. He plowed his hands into her hair, pushing the rubber band free before tangling his fingers into the long tresses. There was no escape, she realized as he kissed her.

Antonio easily broke through her resistance as his tongue plunged into her mouth. She had physically ached from the loss of this passion. This was what she wanted back in her life, whatever the consequences.

Isabella surrendered and sagged against Antonio. She grabbed onto his shoulders, needing to hold something solid as her world spun crazily. Her hands skimmed his back and she clutched his shirt, bunching the fine linen in her fists.

Antonio's growl of triumph vibrated deep in his chest. The sound tugged deep inside her as she rolled her hips restlessly against him.

Isabella skimmed her hands over his broad chest, shoving his tie to one side. Her fingers fumbled with urgency against his strong neck before she speared her fingers through his thick hair. She ground her mouth against his, craving another taste of him.

Antonio groaned with pleasure as he delved his tongue past her lips. Her skin tingled with anticipation as she drew him in deeper. He dominated and conquered her mouth, leaving her breathless.

He leaned in and trapped her firmly against the window with his body. Isabella wanted to feel his hands all over her, wanted him to pleasure her as only he could. She rubbed her hips against his thick arousal, teasing him until his fingers clamped down on her waist. Antonio held her still, the strength and size of his hands sending a thrill down her spine.

Tearing his mouth away from hers, Antonio muttered something in Italian against her cheek that she didn't catch. He slanted his mouth against her throat and laved her heated skin with the tip of his tongue. Isabella fisted his hair and tilted her head back, offering him free rein.

As he caressed her neck with his lips Antonio brushed his fingertips against the hem of her T-shirt. Her breath caught in her throat as he glided his hands along her ribcage. Isabella pressed her hands flat on the window behind her, arching her spine, brazenly offering herself to Antonio as he grazed his fingers along the underside of her breasts.

Isabella swallowed hard as impatient need swirled inside her. Her legs trembled, her heart raced and desire clawed through her. She felt a hint of feminine pride as she watched his chest rise and fall rapidly as he fought for restraint. She knew then that he too felt the relentless compulsion, but he was trying to control it.

Isabella didn't want him to hold back. She needed Antonio to act on the wild desire that pulsated between them. She had to relive this feeling one more time.

She reached for Antonio's necktie and pulled it free. The silk hadn't landed on the floor before she tore at his shirt buttons, her fingers scrabbling with haste. She parted the fine linen, exposing Antonio's golden-brown chest. Clutching the shirt with both hands, Isabella dragged him closer, until the hard, aching tips of her breasts rubbed against the coarse black hair on his chest.

Isabella moaned as her nipples tightened against the soft cotton of her T-shirt. She wanted to feel his skin on her. Isabella shoved Antonio's shirt off his powerful shoulders, desperate to feel more of him. She wanted all of him.

"Say my name," he said roughly as he dragged her shirt up.

"Anto—" Isabella frowned, momentarily confused, until it dawned on her why he'd made that request. Did he believe she was thinking of Giovanni? She gasped against his mouth as hurt ricocheted inside her. Flattening her hands against his hard chest, she tried to push him away. "How dare you?" she said in a whisper.

"Your eyes were closed," he mocked. "And you weren't saying anything. I wanted to make sure you knew which brother you were kissing."

Her palms stung with the need to slap him hard. She had surrendered to Antonio against her better judgment, but he'd seen it as another way to insult her. She shook with anger as she curled her hands into fists. "Get away from me."

Antonio ignored her command and grabbed her wrists. She tried to break his hold but he easily raised her hands high above her head. He held her captive and she was at his mercy.

He leaned against her until his body was flush with hers. As much as she tried to fight it her body softened, welcoming him closer. His heat, his scent clouded her mind. The fierce pounding of her heart matched his.

"Were you thinking of him when you kissed me?" he asked in a drawl.

"No!" How could he think that? Couldn't he tell that all she wanted—all she had ever wanted—was him? She rocked against Antonio in an attempt to break free.

He captured her earlobe between his teeth. Isabella stilled as the nip sent a shower of sensation through her veins.

"Does he kiss like me?" he whispered in her ear. "Do we taste the same?"

Fury and lust whipped through her body. "You are disgusting." But most of all she was disgusted with herself. How could she respond to his touch so immediately while he said those hurtful words?

"Did you think of me when he was deep inside you?"

"Stop it!"

Antonio rested his forehead against hers. "I want to erase his claim on you," he confessed in a harsh whisper. "I want to take you to bed and make you forget Gio."

"I am not going to bed with you." She wanted to. Oh, how she wanted to drag him to his bed and make love all night long. But her heart would never recover. Isabella knew he would kick her out in the morning. The hurt, the pain of his rejection, would overshadow any pleasure he'd given her.

He didn't reply. Instead he dipped his head and trailed a row of soft kisses along the line of her clenched jaw. Isabella shut her eyes, her anticipation escalating as intense sensations billowed through her.

"I mean it, *Antonio*," she said, emphasizing his name. "I will not sleep with a man who thinks so little of me."

She felt his mouth curve into a smile. "Bella, we both know that's not true."

He was right, and his certainty was humiliating.

Antonio knew the power he held over her. One touch, one kiss and she wouldn't deny him. She would make love to him anywhere, at any time. And she had.

Antonio met her gaze, his dark eyes blurred with desire. "I only have to say the word and you would surrender completely."

Her skin flushed hotly. The only thing that kept her glaring right back at him was the reminder that there had been times when *he* had surrendered. When she had tapped into his fantasies. Once she'd had this power over *him*.

Antonio claimed her mouth with his. Just when she thought she couldn't take it anymore Antonio captured her tongue and drew on it hard. She moaned as she felt the pull go deep into her pelvis. Pleasure spilt through her.

"So responsive," he murmured against her mouth. "You must have learned a lot in my brother's bed."

She turned her head sharply and avoided his mouth. If only she could avoid his words. She couldn't protect herself from his anger. From his accusations. He wanted to get close enough so she could share his pain, but she suspected he was getting caught in his own trap. And, even though he treated her like the enemy, she still clung to him.

"I could take you right here against this window, but I can't be sure whose name you'll cry out."

Isabella flinched. She desperately wanted to retaliate. Make wild comparisons between Antonio and his brother. Call out Giovanni's name. She wanted to hurt him so badly he would never recover.

But she wouldn't. His torment was hers. She was still

in love with Antonio and had already caused him so much pain. She couldn't forgive herself for that.

"Are you done with this little demonstration?" she asked brokenly as she fought back the tears. "I'm tired and I want to go to bed. *Alone.*"

"You don't have to worry about that, Bella." Antonio slowly let go of her hands and took a step back. "What we had was good, but I've never been interested in my brother's cast-offs."

That burned. Isabella bolted away from him. Her movements were awkward and shaky as she walked across the room and grabbed her backpack. She wanted to keep walking. Out the door. Out of Antonio's life.

Let him think the worst of her. It didn't matter anymore. They had no future together. She had already wasted so much time trying to get him back. What they'd had was a dream, and the beauty and magic were fading every minute she tried to hold onto it.

"Leave and I'll drag you back in here," Antonio warned. "You are carrying the Rossi heir."

How could he be like this? So ruthless and hard after the kiss they'd just shared? And why couldn't she be just as unemotional?

She whirled around and glared at Antonio. His shirt was unbuttoned, his hair mussed, but he still had a commanding presence. He was in control while she felt like she was being tossed from one crashing wave after another.

"I was in love with you," she announced bitterly.

Antonio didn't show any sign of surprise. That rankled. He knew how she'd felt. He had always known. And it didn't make a difference.

"I was so deeply and so foolishly in love," she said. "It was the reason that I put my future on hold."

"I never asked you to do that."

"I changed the course of my life to be with you," she said as she walked across the length of the room to the doorway, avoiding Antonio. "And right at this moment I regret it."

His eyes glittered with anger. "You regret getting caught. You didn't expect Gio to tell me the truth."

"I regret *you*," she retaliated. She wasn't sure if it was true. Her emotions were running high. Frustration billowed through her chest. "You were the biggest mistake of my life. But don't worry, Antonio. I learn from my mistakes and I never repeat them."

CHAPTER SIX

Mornings were the worst.

Isabella groaned as she sat on the bathroom floor, her bare legs sprawled on the cold linoleum. She had to get up and get dressed. She wished she could sit here until her stomach settled, but she didn't have the luxury of time.

How was she going to get through this pregnancy? Hell, how was she going to get through this morning?

Another question slipped into her mind and she couldn't push it away fast enough.

How was she going to be a mother?

A heavy ache settled in her chest. She was scared of going through this alone. She wasn't ready to be a parent. A single mom. Isabella had always assumed she would be a mother one day. Far, far in the future. But in the meantime she'd had other plans. A few goals she'd wanted to accomplish. She had promised her mother.

Isabella weakly closed her eyes. If her mother were alive, she would be devastated by the news. Before Jody Williams had become ill she had done everything possible to give her daughter the opportunities she hadn't had. Isabella remembered the litany of advice and warnings. *Finish college before you have a child... Never rely on a man... Protect yourself...*

At the time Isabella had thought her mother had a bitter view of the world, but her negativity was understandable. Jody's dreams had been cut short when she'd become a teen mother. Everyone had turned her back on her. The first one to walk away had been the father of her child. *Stay away from the rich ones*, her mother had said frequently. *They have so many choices that they don't know how to commit.*

Isabella wiped a tear from the corner of her eye. She had been so certain that nothing could sidetrack her from her dreams. No man would stand in her way.

She had been so arrogant. So naïve. But she couldn't dwell on that anymore. Now she needed to protect herself and her child. She would be as strong and resilient as her mother had been for her.

She slowly stood, her legs shaky and weak. Her stomach churned and she tried desperately to ignore it. Clutching the rim of the sink, Isabella turned on the faucet and rinsed her mouth out with water. She splashed her face and glanced up in the mirror.

Her hair, which had once been her glory, fell limp against her shoulders. She was pale, her eyes dull and her lips colorless. She saw the strain tightening her features. She was a mess. It would take hours to make her appearance presentable. Normal. Even longer until she felt that way.

The morning sickness was worse today, Isabella decided as she reached for a towel. Was it from the lack of sleep? The stress? Why did it have to be today, when she needed to be strong as she faced Antonio and demanded her plane ticket? She couldn't show any weakness around him.

"Bella?"

Panic radiated from her chest to her arms and legs when she heard the authoritative knock on her bedroom door. *No!* He couldn't come in here. He couldn't see her like this. Bella propelled herself forward just as Antonio entered her bedroom.

She slammed the bathroom door closed but it was already too late. He had seen her. He had stopped in mid-step at the sight of her in a T-shirt and panties. She could only hope her skimpy sleepwear had distracted him from the dark circles under her eyes and the greenish cast of her complexion.

"Why are you hiding in the bathroom?" he demanded.

"I'm not dressed," she said.

"I'm well aware of that." His voice was close and she knew he stood on the other side of the door. "But I've seen you in a lot less. Come out."

"No." She rested her head against the door and fought the urge to slump to the floor. Her body was punishing her for the sudden movement and the jolt of panic.

"Is this because of last night?"

"Maybe." She took a few shallow breaths but her stomach still threatened to revolt.

"I told you, I'm not interested in my brother's castoffs," he taunted.

"Yes," she said, and swallowed hard, "you really proved that last night."

Antonio sighed and she pictured him raking his hair with his hand. "We need to meet with the doctor in an hour."

"That isn't necessary," she insisted. "I've been to a doctor recently and everything is fine."

"You may be okay with that but I want a second opinion. Why wouldn't you want to visit one of Italy's top obstetricians?"

Isabella's shoulders sagged in defeat. When Antonio explained it like that, she really didn't have a reason to decline. "I'll be ready soon." *If she was lucky.*

"You still need to eat breakfast."

The idea made her gag, which she tried to cover up with a loud cough. "No, thanks. I'm not hungry."

"Then eat dry toast. Or have a cappuccino."

She grimaced as she pictured the milky drink. Oh, God. She was going to be sick again.

"Bella?" He turned the doorknob.

"Fine," she said in a high, urgent voice. She didn't care how it sounded. The less she argued, the faster he would leave.

She fought against the nausea, her skin going hot and cold, as she listened to Antonio's familiar footsteps. When he closed the bedroom door she ran to the toilet and vomited.

That had been too close, she decided as she lay on the floor. If Antonio had known she had been sick he wouldn't have left her alone. While she wouldn't mind having someone take care of her, Antonio would have seen how weak she felt. She couldn't allow that.

She was no longer his lover and was now a hindrance. An inconvenient obstacle. She was the reason he wouldn't inherit what was rightfully his. Isabella couldn't forget that. If she showed a chink in her armor, if she revealed any vulnerability, Antonio would take advantage. It was his nature.

She had to get out of here.

And I will once I've visited the doctor, Isabella thought as she turned on the shower. She would demand a plane ticket and deal with any paperwork through the lawyers. She couldn't be around Antonio anymore. Especially after last night. Because if he didn't suspect already Antonio would soon realize that *he* was her only weakness. And he would use that information ruthlessly to get what he wanted.

Weak and shaky, it took her much longer to get ready than she'd anticipated. She pulled her damp hair back in a tight ponytail and dressed simply in a gray T-shirt, jeans and her scuffed-up flats. Looking in the mirror, she wondered how she'd ever gained Antonio's attention. She wasn't beautiful or sexy. There was nothing special about how she looked. She had nothing to offer someone as rich and worldly as Antonio.

Maybe he'd slept with her because she was different from the women he normally had in his life. She was earthy compared to those glamorous creatures. Isabella grabbed her backpack and strode across the bedroom. Or maybe it was because she'd made it known that she found him desirable. That was more likely. Isabella swung open the door and jumped back when she saw Antonio standing in front of her.

"Here—eat this." He offered a piece of dry toast.

Isabella reared her head back. The bread did nothing to whet her appetite. "I was heading for the dining room."

"Where you would have found an excuse not to eat breakfast," he predicted. "I know you don't believe me, but you will feel better after you've eaten."

Once she would have found comfort in the fact that

Antonio knew her so well. Now it made her feel vulnerable. She snatched the toast from his hand, deciding she needed to pick her battles. She didn't want to argue with him when she needed to get her plane ticket.

She looked at the toast with hesitation and then glanced up at Antonio when she noticed he wasn't walking away. "Are you just going to stand there and watch me eat?"

"It's the only way I'll know you've been fed."

Isabella frowned. Why did he care? "I can take care of myself."

"I've already caught you once when you fainted," he reminded her as he crossed his arms as if ready for battle. "I don't want to make it a habit."

"It won't be," she said as she leaned against the wall and nibbled on the toast. She hated being an inconvenience. Or, worse, an obligation. She always toughed it out on her own, took care of her problems alone, and promptly repaid any favor or debt. She didn't accept charity and she wasn't going to start now.

"Can you give me the address of the doctor's office?" she asked Antonio, avoiding his intent gaze as she took another bite of toast.

"No need. I'm coming with you."

She almost choked on the bread. "Why? It's a simple examination and a blood test. You don't need to be there."

"Why do you hate the idea so much?" he asked, and his gaze narrowed on her face. "Do you have something to hide?"

"No, but I don't need to be watched like a hawk." She wanted to handle this alone. Antonio would immediately take over and she knew she would lose the power struggle.

"We'll need to do a DNA test to prove paternity," he explained.

"I'll sign a release form and the lab will send you the results," she promised as she finished the last of the toast. "Or are you afraid I might tamper with the procedure?"

"Are you always this suspicious when someone tries to help you?" he asked as he arched an eyebrow.

"Yes." Because no one offered help unless there was an agenda. The last time she'd accepted assistance she had become a pawn in Giovanni's games.

Antonio took a step forward. "Then you need to work on that, because from now on I'm going to be with you every step of the way."

She should take that as a threat, but she felt her body soften and warm at the promise. "We both know that's the last thing you want to do," she muttered.

"You are carrying the Rossi heir." He gestured at her stomach. "This is my concern as much as yours."

Isabella automatically wrapped her arms around her belly. "You can't possibly want to have anything to do with me or my child. You think this baby is proof that I cheated on you."

"I wouldn't blame a child for his parents' sins."

Isabella stilled as Antonio's words stung. She took a deep breath. "I'm not willing to test that out."

Antonio flattened his hands against the wall as a dark, unpredictable energy swirled around him. "Do you think that I'm the kind of man who would mistreat a child?" he asked in a low, biting tone.

Her instincts said no. She knew Antonio would use

all his power and resources to protect a child. But this was Giovanni's baby. She didn't know much about the history between the brothers, but she knew it was filled with pain and betrayal. Could Antonio separate his feelings for Giovanni from the feelings he had for the baby?

"I don't know," she admitted, tilting her head up to meet his angry gaze. "I've never seen you around kids."

"I haven't seen *you* around children, either," he said as he leaned in, "but I know enough about you to know that you would be a good mother. I don't need a blood test to know that this child is family."

Family. She really wanted her child to grow up with a sense of belonging and surrounded by unconditional love. Her mother had given her those things, but there had been times when she had wanted acceptance from the family that had shunned her. There had been times when Isabella had wondered what was wrong with her that her relatives should withhold their love and approval.

"I take care of my family," Antonio said, his voice strong and clear, "and I will take care of this child."

Isabella blinked slowly as she listened to his vow. Why was he claiming this child? She hadn't expected that. But then why would she? Her own father hadn't claimed *her*. Giovanni had only claimed his baby because he could use the information to hurt Antonio. What did Antonio expect to get from all this? What was his end game? Whatever it was, she didn't think she could afford the price.

"My baby doesn't need your financial support," she declared huskily, and tried to move away. Antonio settled his hand against her shoulder and she stopped.

"It's not just money," he explained. "Your child will

one day head the Rossi empire. He will be part of this world. He needs me to guide him through it," Antonio said as he removed his hand from her shoulder. "Unless you think you're up for the challenge?"

Isabella felt her skin flush. She was an outsider while Antonio's family ruled high society. "Who says my child will want this world?"

"That should be his decision, not yours. Your child will need to be groomed from the beginning. He will need to attend the best schools, train—"

"I can provide that now. I am *not* a disadvantage to my baby," she insisted, hating how her voice shook.

She was surprised when Antonio hooked his finger under her chin and guided her face up so she could look into his eyes. "Your baby is already lucky to have you as a mother," he assured her softly. "You are very nurturing and affectionate."

Maybe too much so. During their affair she hadn't held back on her embraces and caresses. She'd always been touching Antonio. Holding on. Clinging. It had led him to think that she was like that with everyone.

"But you don't think I can give this child the sort of life that befits a Rossi heir?" she said.

Antonio dropped his hand and took a step back. "That's where I can help."

It was too good to be true. There must be some strings attached to his offer. An expectation of good behavior or a short expiration date.

"For how long? Until it's no longer in your interest? When you start a family of your own?" With that fiancée of his. The thought of the other woman made Isabella want to crumple up in pain. She'd seen pictures of the sophisticated lady. She was beautiful, from a prominent Italian family. She would be an asset to Antonio while Isabella had been a liability.

"I am committed to being in this child's life. From this moment on. Whenever I am needed I'll be there."

"Antonio, you don't know the first thing about commitment."

"How can you say that? I have always met my obligations. I have a duty to—"

She raised her hand to stop him. "I am *not* your obligation and you have *no* duty to my child," she said fiercely. "I am solely responsible for my baby and I don't want your help."

He gave an arrogant shrug. "Too bad because you already have it."

"Your type of help will be more like interference and influence." She stopped as she thought of her words yesterday. *You have no rights over me or my child.* That was what this was all about. Isabella closed her eyes as anger washed over her. Oh, she was so stupid for not realizing it sooner. "You want to control the power and the money Giovanni gave to me."

"No," he said through clenched teeth.

"Are you worried that I would squander the family fortune? Or that I will abuse my power?" She shook her head. "Don't worry. I didn't ask for this kind of responsibility. I don't even want it. But I'm doing it to protect my child's interests."

"If you don't want the responsibility I can help you with that. If the tests prove that this child is Giovanni's I'll pay you a lump sum in exchange for your interest in the Rossi empire. You will have millions more dollars at your fingertips instantly and you won't have to make any business decisions."

Isabella noticed he'd come up with the alternative quickly. It was almost as if he'd been waiting to present it. "And you won't have to deal with me or my baby," she pointed out sweetly.

Antonio's nostrils flared as he reined in his temper. "My commitment to you and the baby would remain the same."

"It's a tempting offer," she said with exaggerated politeness, "but I'll have to think about it."

Isabella turned away as she battled conflicting emotions. She'd known Antonio had an ulterior motive, but she was filled with disappointment because she was right.

She knew better than to accept Antonio's help. He'd said he was fully committed, but what he really meant was that he would be committed until he could get full control of the Rossi money. The minute he got what he wanted Antonio would discard her from his life with the same ruthlessness as before.

"Committed? Yeah, right."

"What was that?" Antonio was right behind her. She felt his heat and his towering strength.

Isabella knew she should let it go, but the anger was building up inside her. She slowly turned around, wondering if this was the smartest move, and confronted Antonio. "I think your definition of commitment is different from mine. You couldn't commit to me, but now you'll pledge a lifetime of commitment to a child?"

Antonio clenched his teeth and a muscle bunched in his jaw. "You question my ability to commit when *you* are the one who cheated?" His harsh voice was almost a whisper.

"I didn't cheat," she said with a weary sigh. "Not

that it matters. If Giovanni hadn't come up with that story I'm sure you would have found another reason to dump me."

Antonio's eyes darkened as tension crackled around them. "That's not true."

"It is. Men like you don't *do* relationships." She had been warned, but she hadn't listened. She'd thought what she'd had with Antonio had been different. Special. That it would beat the odds.

"Men like me?"

"You have money, power and so many choices." And she'd had nothing to offer to make him want to stay. "Why make a commitment when something new and exciting, something better, is just around the corner?"

Antonio grabbed her wrist and pulled her close. "I wanted you and only you."

She believed him. But she also believed the feeling had been temporary. "And how does your fiancée feel about that?" Isabella asked as she pulled from his grasp.

"So that is where all this is coming from?" Antonio exhaled sharply and rubbed his hand over his face. "Let me assure you, Bella, I do *not* have a fiancée."

"Isn't that just a technicality?" she asked as she rubbed her wrist, hating how her pulse skipped and her skin tingled from his touch. "You haven't put a ring on her finger yet, but there is an agreement."

"I was engaged, but that was before I met you."

He had been engaged? Maybe he did know how to commit, but just not to her. "To the woman they mentioned in the news? Aida?"

Antonio nodded. "Her parents were good friends with mine. It was to be an arranged marriage."

Isabella's mouth parted in surprise. "Why would you

do something like that?" Antonio was the most sexual man she knew. Passionate. He would have suffered in a paper marriage.

"We came from the same world, had the same interests, and the marriage would have been advantageous for both families. Aida would have made a good wife."

Aida clearly offered everything she could not. Isabella tried not to think about that. "If it was such a good match, why aren't you married?"

He rubbed the back of his neck and looked away. "Before we announced our engagement Aida decided she couldn't bear the idea of getting married to me when she had fallen in love with Gio."

"Oh." Isabella's eyes widened. "Is *that* why you and your brother were estranged?"

Antonio shook his head. "Gio never knew, thank God. He had no interest in Aida. She might as well have been invisible to him."

Isabella wondered if this was why Antonio was so quick to assume she'd used him to get to Giovanni. His own fiancée had rejected him for his brother. It would have been hard to get over that, arranged marriage or not. "I'm sorry."

"Why? I wasn't in love with Aida, but I would have taken my wedding vows seriously. I know how to make a commitment and how to honor it." He took a step back and glanced at his watch. "That's all you need to know."

"No, it's not," she said with exasperation. Typical of Antonio. If he felt he'd revealed too much, or if it veered into uncomfortable territory, he shut the conversation down immediately.

"Then let me be clear," he said in a clipped tone. "It doesn't matter whether you accept your inheritance or let me buy you out. This is still Gio's baby and I'm still going to be part of this child's life. Get used to it."

He was in hell.

The white walls of the doctor's office were closing in on him. His hands were cold, his chest clenched and he wanted to walk away. Instead he stood by the door, arms folded, as the amplified sounds of an infant's heartbeat filled the examination room.

He watched Isabella as she listened. Her face softened and she pressed her lips together as she listened to her baby. The child might have been unplanned, but Isabella had already bonded with this child and wanted it fiercely.

The ultrasound technician invited him to come closer. Antonio declined with a shake of his head and didn't move. He felt like he shouldn't be there, that he was intruding on a very private moment. He'd promised to look after Isabella and her child, but that didn't erase the fact that he was standing in for his brother. *Again.*

And Isabella had made it clear she didn't want him around. Her instincts were right on target. He *was* doing all this to gain control of her. She wasn't going to give up her fortune—that had been a long shot. Which meant marriage. He could make her fall in love with him, but that wouldn't be enough. He needed to demonstrate that he could accept the baby as his own.

"Everything looks fine and your baby has a strong heartbeat," the lab tech said as she got up from her chair. "You can get dressed now and go to the lab to get your blood taken."

"How long will it take to get the results?" Antonio asked.

"I'll ask them to hurry," the woman said as she approached him, "but it can take up to a week."

A week was too long. He wasn't thinking only about the legal aspects of confirming Gio's heir. Having Isabella in his life, in his home, was already placing a strain on his self-control. She had only been under his roof for a few minutes when he had pounced.

He thanked the technician, ignoring the flirty promise that lay beneath her fluttering eyelashes. He closed the door firmly behind her and turned around when he heard Isabella's deep sigh.

"This is why I wanted to come alone to this doctor's appointment."

"Why?" Antonio asked as he watched Isabella sit up and swing her bare legs over the edge of the examination table. "What did I do?"

"She was paying more attention to you than the screen."

"You're exaggerating," he said. Her comment surprised him. Isabella wasn't the jealous type, but then he had never given her reason to worry. His adoration had been painfully obvious.

Isabella hopped down from the table and her paper gown rustled loudly. "I'm going to get dressed."

Antonio retrieved his phone from his jacket and leaned against the door. He scrolled through a few messages before he glanced up again. Isabella was tapping her bare feet impatiently and had her hands on her hips.

"I'd like some privacy."

He raised an eyebrow. This from the woman who had once given him a striptease so erotic that his body still clenched from the memory of it? "You can't be serious."

She glared at him. "Will you at least turn your back?"

"No." He pocketed his phone and crossed his arms. He should probably be a gentleman and allow her to get ready in private, but he didn't like being relegated to the status of an acquaintance. A stranger. They had once been lovers and he didn't want her to forget it.

"Fine. Hold this while I dress." She thrust the ultrasound printout in his hand.

He automatically looked down at the black and white image of Isabella's baby.

Gio's baby.

His fingers pinched the edge of the picture.

Antonio braced himself for searing pain as he stared at the image. But all he felt was curiosity and regret. He wished Isabella were carrying *his* child.

What kind of father would Gio have been? Antonio wondered. Would he have been a disciplinarian, like their father, or would he have been an absent parent? He didn't think Gio would have offered stability or comfort. His brother had been famous for his playboy lifestyle and wouldn't have changed his ways to accommodate a baby.

Antonio, on the other hand, was already prepared to make changes for this child. He frowned at the picture, noticing how small and innocent the baby appeared. He could offer the child a stable environment. Protection. But love? *That* he didn't know.

"Is something wrong?" Isabella asked softly.

Antonio realized he had been staring at the picture all this time. "I think it's a girl," he said gruffly.

"I haven't asked about the sex of the baby," Isabella said. She turned around and walked to the chair that held her clothes. "All I care about is the baby's health."

Antonio glanced at the paper gown that fell onto the

floor. A kick of anticipation heated his blood. His gaze trailed from Isabella's bare feet to her slender legs. He wanted to let his eyes roam, to memorize every line and bend of her body, but that would be dangerous. Antonio knew once he did that he wouldn't be able to keep his hands off Isabella.

"Was your assistant able to find a plane ticket for me?" she asked as she stepped into her panties. The cheap cotton didn't detract from the gentle curve of her hips, and his hands stung with the need to drag it down her thighs.

"Plane ticket?" he asked in a daze. He remembered the warmth and softness of her skin. The way she'd nestled perfectly against him when they slept.

"To Los Angeles," she said as she hooked thin bra straps over her shoulders. "That was the deal."

He watched the muscles in her back move sinuously as she hooked her bra. Her fingers fumbled on the last hook and Antonio stood very still as desire whipped through his body. He wasn't going to offer any assistance. He would not brush her hands away and let his fingers graze her skin as he unhooked the bra and peeled it off…

Antonio cleared his throat. "That was before I knew you were carrying the Rossi heir."

She glanced over her shoulder. "A deal is a deal, Antonio."

He could argue, point out that she had withheld important information. Instead he watched, fixated, as Isabella bent from the waist. Her long blonde hair swayed along her shoulders as she shimmied into her jeans.

"Wait until the results are back?" he suggested. It

wasn't a great idea. For his own preservation it would be better if Isabella was far away.

"There is no need," Isabella said as she hastily put on her shirt. "I know what the results are going to say."

"But you don't know what you plan to do. If you want to support your interest in the Rossi fortune then *you* need to learn the business, too. That means staying here."

"And you're going to teach me? Is that right?" she asked as she straightened the hem of her shirt. "And eventually my child. That way you can wield influence even if you *don't* have all the power."

He gritted his teeth. "Your child needs to grow up here in Rome. She needs to understand where she comes from and who her family is. Then she will know what to do when she takes charge of the family business."

"Heritage?" Isabella paused in slipping her foot into her shoe. "She needs to know her heritage?"

Antonio was surprised by the longing in Isabella's voice. "She can only do that around her remaining family," he added. He needed to keep a close eye on Isabella. The last thing he needed was another man in the picture. Antonio's stomach twisted violently at the thought.

"It's a good point." Isabella said, her gaze on her feet. It was obvious that she was having second thoughts. "I need to think about this."

"Think about it here in Rome," he urged.

She nodded slowly. "I'll stay until the test results are ready."

"Good." Antonio felt a hint of relief. He had a week to seduce her. Considering their history, she would capitulate sooner than that.

Isabella reached for the sonogram printout. "Once

we're done here I'll move into a hotel. I don't have the money right now, but maybe I can work something out with the lawyers dealing with the will."

Hotel? He couldn't let that happen. "I have no problem with you staying in my apartment."

"I don't want to take advantage of your hospitality," she replied. "I think I've already overstayed my welcome."

"Not at all. In fact I won't be in Rome for the rest of the week. I have business to attend to in Paris," Antonio lied.

Isabella bit her bottom lip. "I don't know…"

"Stay. I insist." His strategy would only work if she remained in his home and in his control. "It will put my mind at ease knowing that you are cared for while I'm gone."

"Okay, thank you," she said with a grateful smile. "By the time you come back I'm sure I'll have made my decision."

And Antonio was determined to do everything in his power to have the decision work in his favor.

CHAPTER SEVEN

FIVE days later Isabella sat in Maria Rossi's grand home just outside Rome. She perched on the edge of a sofa and silently accepted a fine china teacup. She winced when the cup rattled on the saucer.

Do not drop it. The tea set looked like it had cost more than her entire college tuition fees. The rug beneath her feet had to be obscenely expensive. It didn't take any expertise in antiques to know that everything in the room was priceless. She needed to keep her hands in her lap and refrain from making any sudden movements.

She and Antonio's mother made an odd tea party. Maria wore a silk dress and pearls, while Isabella wore dime-store denim and cotton. Her skin prickled as she remembered the disapproving look from the butler when she had arrived. She fought the urge to tug at her skirt, which was several inches above her bare knees.

Isabella wasn't sure what the protocol was for tea, so she waited for the older woman to drink from her own cup, then took a polite sip from her tea and carefully set the cup and saucer down gently on the table in front of her.

"It was kind of you to invite me to your house, Mrs.

Rossi," Isabella said, hoping to get through this quickly. "I'm wondering what the occasion is."

"Please, call me Maria."

The woman must want something if she was trying to be friendly, and Isabella felt a stab of guilt. She didn't know anything about Maria Rossi. It was possible that she was a kind soul who only turned into a lioness when she felt her family was being threatened. It was highly unlikely, but anything was possible.

"It must be important," Isabella continued. "I know you aren't entertaining while you're in mourning."

"This isn't entertaining," Maria corrected her. "You're practically family."

She was glad she wasn't holding the china cup when Maria said that. Unsure how to respond, Isabella smiled tightly and glanced around the room. Her eyes bulged when she recognized a painting from one of her art history classes.

Her fingers tightened and she pushed her elbows in closer to her body. She'd never seen a home like this, even when she'd used to clean houses with her mother. It made her uncomfortable. Nervous.

"I understand you took a DNA test to establish paternity?" Maria said.

Isabella slowly returned her attention to Antonio's mother. "Just a formality." She was sensitive about the fact that she had been made to take the blood test. She wasn't a slut who didn't know the father of her baby.

"Have you received the results?"

Please. Isabella narrowed her eyes at Maria. She'd got the call this morning and an hour later had been summoned to the Rossi family estate. That was no coincidence. Maria had probably known the results before she had. "Yes, I have."

"And?" Maria prompted as she took another sip of tea.

Isabella took a deep breath, knowing that Maria was going to be a part of her life once she gave the answer whether she liked it or not. "Giovanni is the father."

To her surprise Maria's eyes dulled and a sad smile flickered across her lips. "It's a shame he will never be able to see his child," she said softly.

Isabella tried to remember that this woman was grieving for her son. Maria had been rude and hurtful to her, but she was suffering. Isabella remembered how it had felt when her mother had died, and tried to find some compassion.

At least Maria had Antonio, Isabella reminded herself. She wouldn't feel lost and alone. Unlike her, Maria had other family to rely on.

Maria regained her composure and took another fortifying sip of her tea. "Anything else?" she asked briskly.

Isabella wasn't sure what she was asking. Did Maria know something she didn't?

Isabella shrugged. "Antonio thinks it's a girl."

"I'm only going by the ultrasound." Antonio said as he entered the room.

Isabella heart lurched when she heard Antonio's deep voice. She whirled around and saw him striding toward her. He was a commanding figure, his confidence and energy crackling into the stifling atmosphere. Although he was dressed casually, in faded jeans and a long-sleeved shirt, Antonio looked like he ruled the world.

She didn't know why she had such a fierce reaction

from seeing him again. It had only been five days. It wasn't as if she'd been out of contact with him. She had spoken to him daily on the phone while he was gone. He had also sent links throughout each day to websites about pregnancy and maternal health. Only this morning she had discovered he had been in contact with the doctor's office, asking advice about her debilitating morning sickness.

This was a side to Antonio she hadn't expected, Isabella realised as she watched Antonio greet his mother with brief kiss on the cheek. He was her fantasy lover and a fascinating man—but thoughtful and protective…?

She saw Antonio pause as a shadow passed along his face. Isabella immediately knew he had caught a glimpse of Giovanni's photo next to Maria's chair.

He was being a picture of strength and power for the sake of his mother and the employees who depended on him, but she knew he was hiding his own suffering. Giovanni had been his brother. Isabella wanted to offer him comfort, but he was too proud for that. She would lighten his burden if she could, but Antonio wasn't someone who shared his thoughts or his pain.

Oh, damn. Isabella closed her eyes weakly as the truth hit her. She was still in love with Antonio. She had never stopped loving him. For months she had wished for reconciliation, with the loss of what she'd had with Antonio almost driving her mad. She'd tried to be practical, tried to move on, but she couldn't extinguish that whisper of hope.

Rubbing her aching head, Isabella wondered if she'd ever learn. This was why she needed to keep her distance. She wasn't going to start up again with Antonio.

It didn't matter how much they wanted each other or how much she loved him. Nothing would change the fact that he still believed she had been unfaithful.

"What are you doing here?" Isabella blurted out.

Antonio faced her, his gaze warming as it traveled from her face to her bare legs and back to her eyes. "I was going to ask you the same."

"I invited her to tea," Maria explained. "She told me the blood test results are in and Gio is the father."

Isabella saw a stealthy look pass between mother and son. She didn't know what it meant. Had they seriously questioned the paternity of her child?

"And," Maria continued, "I was hoping to know what her plans are now."

The two looked at her expectantly and Isabella felt her nervousness spike. She knew they weren't going to like her decision, but she had to be strong.

"I'm leaving Rome. Today," she added. She had to leave before Antonio discovered her weak points. Had to get out before he talked about family and heritage. Before he made seductive promises he had no way of keeping.

She sensed Maria's disappointment. She tried not to look directly at Antonio. She couldn't determine his re-action. Was he surprised? Did he know how much she had wrestled with this decision? Had he been hoping she would stay?

Maria frowned. "But…"

Isabella raised her hand to hold off any arguments. "I plan to visit Rome frequently. I want my child to know his or her family. But it's best for me to return to Los Angeles and finish my degree."

Maria tilted her head to look at Antonio. "Talk to

her," she said in Italian. "Take her into the gardens and convince her to stay in Rome."

Isabella lowered her head and kept her gaze on her hands. Did Maria think she didn't understand *any* Italian? How did she think she had been able to live in Rome all these months? She pressed her lips before she corrected the older woman. She knew some Italian, but not enough to speak fluently.

Isabella's pulse quickened as Antonio approached her. She glanced up and her heart did a slow tumble when she saw his weary face. She didn't think she'd ever seen him like this. She wanted to smooth away the lines and hold him tight.

"Bella, let's discuss your travel arrangements," he said in English. "Would you like to join me in the gardens?"

Isabella nodded and rose from her seat. She quietly followed him to a door that led out to the magnificent garden. It was as large as a public park, artfully designed with statues and fountains. The lush green lawn was beautifully maintained, and contrasted against the crimson and gold leaves on the large, solid trees.

She shouldn't be doing this, Isabella thought as she walked alongside Antonio. She was obediently following him just to *be* with him. Her chest tightened as she realized this was the last time they would be alone together. Instead of getting closer, she needed to start creating distance.

"You don't need to pretend, Antonio," she said. "I understood what your mother told you."

"I know," he said with a hint of a smile. "But I didn't want to have this conversation in front of her."

"There's nothing to talk about. I thought about staying here in Rome, so my child would know his family and his heritage, but I think it's best for me to return to Los Angeles and finish my college degree."

"You can always finish your degree here."

She shook her head. "My Italian isn't good enough."

"Those are obstacles we can easily overcome. Tell me what you need and I'll make it happen."

Isabella stared at the pale stonework under her feet. No one had offered that kind of support for her while she'd pursued her education. She had done it all on her own. She was proud of her accomplishments, but she'd love to share her future ups and downs with Antonio. Have someone at her side during the journey.

But she couldn't rely on him. If she accepted his help he would expect something in return. Something like allegiance and obedience when it came to matters concerning the Rossi fortune.

"I appreciate the offer," she said woodenly. "I really do. But—"

"What is the real reason you're leaving Rome?" he interrupted. "It's not because you want to continue your education. The academic year has already started and you can't re-enrol for another couple of months. So what is the urgency?"

"Once I make a decision I act immediately."

"No, that's not it." He dismissed her answer with the flick of his hand. "You're leaving because of me."

"You are so—" She stopped herself. What did it matter if he knew how she felt? "Okay, fine. *Yes*, Antonio. It's best for me to leave Rome because of *you*. You think I cheated on you. I gave you no reason to be jealous, and there is no evidence that I cheated, but you're determined to believe the worst about me."

He took a deep breath. "I regret letting Giovanni get between us."

Isabella stopped walking and closed her eyes as old pain washed over her. "But you believed him. You *still* believe him."

Antonio took a step closer. "If I could do it all over again I would do it differently," he said softly. "I should have confronted you. I should have told you about the history between Gio and me. I regret allowing his accusations to ruin what we had."

Isabella noticed he no longer called it Gio's *confession*. She wondered if she was investing too much significance in Antonio's word choice. She opened her eyes and turned to him. "Do you believe me? That I was faithful?"

She saw the struggle in his eyes before he answered. "I want to," he answered slowly. "I'm trying to believe it."

But he couldn't. Disappointment welled up inside her. "Why can't you? What is it about me that makes it so hard to believe?"

He shook his head and tossed his hands up in frustration. "I don't know."

Isabella pressed her lips together as she considered a few possibilities. "Is it because I wasn't a virgin when I met you?"

"No!" Antonio looked surprised by the suggestion.

She squinted as she watched his face. "Or because we fell into bed the day we met?"

"No…"

She heard the moment's hesitation. "Don't you *dare*." She pressed her finger against his chest. "Don't tarnish that memory."

"I'm not," he insisted. "You are bold and passionate. Adventurous and trusting. I'd like to think you were only that way with me."

"I have never fallen that hard or that fast for anyone," Isabella said fiercely, and immediately dropped her hand. She took a step back and pursed her lips. She felt exposed and uncertain, but Antonio needed to hear this. He had to understand just how important he was to her. "And I never will again."

His eyes darkened. "Because you regret it?"

"No," she said, realizing he had gotten it all wrong. "Because the next time it won't be *you*."

Antonio stilled. He didn't speak or move. He stared at her with quiet intensity.

"You know what?" she said, feeling foolish as a blush crept up her cheeks. "It doesn't matter anymore. For one reason or another you can't believe that I was faithful. Tonight I'm out of here and I will be just a memory."

Her words jerked him out of his stupor. "About that…"

She didn't like the sound of that. "About what?"

"Bella…" he said softly.

"No." He wasn't going to give her the ticket. She shook her head and sliced her hands in the air in case she wasn't getting her point across. "No, no, *no*. You promised."

He bent his head and shoved his hands in his pockets. "I'm aware of that."

She pressed her hands against her head as frustration billowed through her. "I need to get back to where I belong. To be in familiar and comfortable surroundings. I have some big changes ahead of me and I need to be ready."

"I understand. I think it's the nesting instinct. But that shouldn't occur until around the fifth month of pregnancy."

Isabella forgot what she'd been going to say next. She stared at Antonio as if he was speaking a different language. "What are you talking about?"

"It's in this book I'm reading about pregnancy and labor."

"You're reading a book about *pregnancy*?" His admission astounded her. She hadn't expected him to have an interest. When they had visited the obstetrician it had looked as if Antonio had wanted to be anywhere but in that examination room. "If you understand why I need to leave, then why are you asking me to stay?"

Antonio swallowed, opened his mouth and stopped. He clenched his jaw and looked away.

Isabella watched with growing concern. She had never seen him hesitant.

"Antonio?" Isabella prompted. "What is it?"

"Gio left a mess." The words came out in a rush. "It's a nightmare."

"Okay." What did that have to do with her? Did it have something to do with the will? Wouldn't the lawyers inform her if so?

He squeezed his eyes shut and raked his hand through his hair. "Never mind. Forget I said anything."

She watched Antonio walk away abruptly, his shoulders stooped as if he was carrying the weight of the world. He was a dark, solitary figure among the bright colors of the garden.

He wasn't *really* alone, she told herself.

But who was there for him?

He was grieving for his brother, but he couldn't show

it while he took care of everyone else. His mother was leaning on him and no one was offering support while he had to move into his brother's role. He'd almost swallowed his pride and asked her to stay.

But why? Why *her*? Was it because there was no one else? He didn't trust her. He still suspected the worst of her. She was not the ideal candidate to stay by his side.

Damn. She wanted to stomp her foot. Why did he have to do this to her? Now? She was so close to leaving. She was almost home.

It wasn't like he'd asked her to bed. He was simply asking for support, right? She could do that. She wanted to do that.

"Antonio, just ask," she called out.

He stopped but didn't turn around. "I understand if you can't," he replied stiffly. "We didn't part on good terms."

Maybe that was why her resolve was weakening. Isabella reached his side and placed her hand on his arm. She couldn't recapture what they'd had, but she could change the ending of their relationship.

"What do you need?"

"You."

Her heart lurched to a stop and then pounded violently. Was he asking for something more than emotional support? Why did she feel that kick of excitement? Almost a week ago she'd told him she wouldn't sleep with a man who didn't trust her. But he wasn't asking to sleep in her bed. He was putting his trust in her hands as he asked for her help.

Isabella nervously swiped her tongue along her bottom lip. "Could you be more specific?"

"I need you at my side," Antonio admitted. He looked

down at her, his eyes stormy and troubled. "Just for a few days while I deal with some competitors. They are circling Rossi Industries hoping to find a weakness. It would help if we looked like a united front. Once that's accomplished then I'll send you home."

Antonio could handle his enemies without her at his side. Isabella suspected this was not really about business or about his mother's request. He was reaching out in his own way. He was taking a risk, knowing she had every right to reject him.

"Do you still want me to stay at your apartment?" she asked calmly as her mind raced. Had Antonio figured out that *he* was her weakness? That, despite her better judgment, she couldn't stay away?

He frowned as though he'd made it obvious. "Yes."

"And I stay in the guestroom?" She didn't know why she'd said that. She didn't want to be there.

"Yes, of course."

She saw that glint in his eye. He had no intention of having her stay in the guestroom. He wanted comfort and support in the most basic form. Antonio wanted a few hours to forget—a few nights where he could lose himself.

And she wanted it, too. She knew his trust in her was fragile, that his motivations had nothing to do with love. She was willing to risk it all if it meant having another night with the man she couldn't stop loving. If he propositioned her, would she reject him? She didn't know.

But she was tired of playing it safe. And she didn't want this affair to have ended when he'd kicked her out of his bed. This time she would walk out when she was ready.

"Sure, Antonio," she said calmly as her heart started to race. "I can stay for three more days. But that's all I can promise."

CHAPTER EIGHT

ISABELLA was relieved when she and Antonio left the Rossi estate a short time later. Once they'd told Antonio's mother that she was extending her stay for a few more days Maria had sent them on their way with barely disguised haste. It was as if Maria had got the result she desired and wanted Isabella gone.

Antonio guided her to his black sports car with a large hand at the small of her back. Her skin tingled from the gentle touch. She knew he didn't mean anything by the gesture, that it was something he did automatically, but she liked it. It made her feel like he was looking after her.

Once Antonio had helped her into his low-slung car, he slid into the driver's seat and checked his watch. "There is a party that I have to attend."

Disappointment filled her. She knew what that meant. When they'd been together Antonio had rarely accepted invitations to a party or event, but there had been times when it was required. He would dress up in a suit or tuxedo, looking so devastatingly handsome that it almost hurt to look at him, and then he would go alone and she would stay at home and wait for him.

In the past Isabella had told herself that she was glad

she hadn't had to go to those parties. She wouldn't know anyone, struggled with the language, and wouldn't feel comfortable in extravagantly luxurious settings. But there had been times when she'd wondered *why* Antonio didn't include her. Was she not good enough to be seen with a Rossi? Had he only wanted her for sex?

She wasn't his lover anymore, but the old insecurities were still there, along with her desire to be with him. She hadn't seen him for days and now he was going out for the night. Only this time she didn't have a claim on him. She wasn't sure she ever had.

But she wasn't going to make the same mistake this time. She was in the city of Rome. There was beauty and excitement all around her. She wasn't going to stay at home in hopes that Antonio would return earlier than planned. She had wasted too much time waiting for him and putting her life on hold. Isabella wanted to make the most of her time in this vibrant city.

"Okay," she said, and she stared straight ahead at the Rome skyline, her gaze focused on the famous dome of St. Peter's Basilica. "I might be home late tonight too."

Antonio started the ignition and paused. "Where are you going?"

Isabella had no idea, but she was sure there were many choices. Maybe she would go to the Piazza di Spagna. She didn't care so long as she wasn't home alone. "I've always wanted to experience Rome at night," she said. "I never really got the chance."

"You were out every night with Gio," he muttered darkly as he sped the car down the wide lane that was flanked by big trees.

"I'm not talking about nightclubs. When you've seen

one, you've seen them all," she said. "I want to explore the city and see a different side of it."

"Can't you postpone that till tomorrow?" Antonio asked as they passed the intimidating iron gates that barred ordinary people from the Rossi world. "I promise I will make it worth the wait and show you Rome under the stars. Tonight I want you to come with me to the party."

"You do? Why?" What had prompted the invitation? Was it because he knew she wasn't going to stay at home and he wanted to keep an eye on her? "I've never gone to a social event with you before."

She knew why. It simply wouldn't have *done* for her to be at his side. He was sophisticated, powerful, part of prestigious family. She, on the other hand, had had no money, no connections, and hadn't known the secret handshakes of high society. She had been a disadvantage. A liability.

"I wanted you all to myself," he confessed. "I know it was selfish but I didn't care."

Isabella jerked her head and stared at Antonio. *That* was why he'd kept her from his world? "I thought it was because you were embarrassed by me."

"Why would you think that? Hell, I would have shown you off, but that would have encouraged an invasion of our privacy. I didn't want anyone intruding on us. But I went too far. It was only this week that I realized how isolated you must have been. That was not my intention."

"I see," she said softly. Why hadn't he told her that earlier? But then, why didn't she insisted that he take her along? Because she had been afraid of making demands. She hadn't felt secure in her relationship with Antonio and hadn't wanted to start a battle.

"Would you *like* to go to this party with me?" Antonio asked as he shifted gears. "I think you'll enjoy it."

She didn't know why he was making the effort now, when she was leaving in a couple of days. Was it an apology or did he really want her to accompany him? She admitted that she was curious about Antonio's life. What was he like when he was around friends and acquaintances? Antonio didn't need to grab the spotlight like his brother, but he wouldn't stay in the shadows, either.

Isabella wanted to accept his invitation, but one thing was holding her back. "I don't have anything to wear. And my hair…" She threaded her fingers along the ends of her hair, certain it was a tumbled mess. She didn't usually style her hair, but she needed to go all out if she wanted to make a good impression.

"You don't need to change," Antonio assured her. "It's a casual party."

"We may have different definitions of *casual*." She remembered Giovanni's circle of friends. *Casual* had meant preparing all day at the spa and wearing outfits that cost the same as a car.

Antonio cast her an appreciative look that made her blush. "Trust me, Bella. You'll fit right in."

Isabella couldn't believe what she was seeing. She couldn't pull her gaze away from Antonio as he leapt into the air. His strong arms were reaching, stretching as he dove for the soccer ball. Isabella's stomach clenched and her skin felt flushed at the sight of his vigor and masculinity. Just when Isabella thought he would grab it, the ball zoomed past him and Antonio tumbled to the ground, rolled and shot to his feet.

A group of young boys cheered as the ball hit the net.

Unbelievable, Isabella thought. She'd never thought Antonio could be having fun at a child's birthday party. He should look out of place among the colorful balloons, party hats and streamers. Instead the children gravitated toward him, eager for his attention. He gave it freely and didn't refuse when several boys asked him to play.

"I have told Antonio a thousand times that he shouldn't let Dino win," said Dino's mother, Fia, as she stood beside Isabella, bouncing baby Giulia on her hip. "But at least he makes my son work for it."

"Maybe soccer isn't Antonio's sport."

"Ha!" Fia said as she tried to give a pacifier to her grumpy baby. "He was one of the best athletes in school. Football, swimming, skiing. He could do it all. He needed a sport for every season to expend his energy."

"I had no idea." She should have known. Antonio was lean and muscular and moved with enviable grace.

"Really?" Fia gave up on the pacifier and shifted baby Giulia onto her other hip. "How long have you known him?"

"A few months." But she hadn't known that he loved sports. There were no trophies or sports equipment in his home. He didn't tell stories about his adventures or his triumphs. Was it really a passion of his or did his abilities come to him so easily that he didn't think much about it? "How about you?"

"My husband has known him since their schooldays, and they've been together through the good times and bad." Fia raised her voice over Giulia's tired cry. "That's why Antonio is Dino's godfather."

Isabella watched Antonio ruffle Dino's hair. His affection for the boy was apparent. "He takes that role seriously."

Fia nodded. "We couldn't have asked for anyone better."

"I've never seen him around children," she murmured as she watched Antonio approach her. Her heart began to beat fast. "He's completely different."

"Not different," Fia said. "More like he's…"

"Unguarded?"

"Exactly." Fia patted Giulia's back but the baby continued to fuss. "I think it's the little one's bedtime."

"Here—let me hold her," Antonio said, and reached out for the baby.

Isabella couldn't hide her surprise as he cradled Giulia in his arms. The baby stopped fussing and stared at Antonio with wide eyes as he spoke softly to her.

"How did you do that?" Isabella asked. She couldn't soothe a baby that quickly even after years of babysitting.

Antonio smiled. "I have this effect on all women."

Fia laughed and lapsed into Italian. She spoke fast and Isabella struggled to keep up with the conversation. Eventually she allowed her gaze to fall on the baby, who was now falling asleep in Antonio's arms.

He was good with children and he liked being around them. How had she not known about this side of Antonio? Before she would have described him as sexy, powerful and remote. But today, as she watched him around his friends and their children, she knew there were many sides of him she had yet to discover. She needed to dig deeper to understand him.

When they left the party it was late at night and the

birthday boy had been asleep for hours. Isabella had enjoyed visiting Antonio's friends. She could tell they were curious about her but they'd made her feel welcome.

She'd noticed how open and relaxed he was with his friends. He was much more formal with his mother, and had been watchful and cautious with his brother. If she wanted to understand Antonio she needed to know the source of the strain between him and his relatives.

But Isabella was hesitant to ask. She bit her bottom lip as Antonio drove back to his apartment in comfortable silence. She didn't want to ruin a perfect evening, but she didn't have a lot of opportunity to find out before she left Rome.

"Antonio, why did you have such a difficult relationship with your brother?"

Antonio frowned, and she felt the mood shift in the small confines of the car. "It's not something I like to talk about."

"I know, but I feel like I'm missing a huge piece of the puzzle." If she had known their history she could have avoided so much heartache. But some instinct warned her that Antonio would have kicked her out sooner or later even without his brother's interference. "What happened between you two?"

Antonio felt Isabella looking at him, curious and expectant. He knew he owed it to her. It wasn't just about him and his brother. Isabella had been affected, too.

"My brother and I were close when we were young," he said, looking straight ahead as he drove through the busy streets. A smile tugged at the corner of his mouth as he remembered how much fun he'd once had with his brother. "My parents didn't have any more children so it was just the two of us. I often heard us described as the heir and the spare."

"Ouch. That's not very nice. Did they said that to *you*?"

He didn't care about the label anymore, but he found Isabella's indignation a comfort. "The servants or guests would say it when they didn't think I understood. Or when they thought I was out of earshot."

"Still, that's not something anyone should say about a child. It's something he'd carry with him. Either he tries to live up to it or fight against it. It would have the power to define him."

"I knew there was some truth to it," he admitted. "My parents loved me, and I was cared for, but Gio was the center of attention. There were times when I felt envious and resentful, but as I got older I realized I was the lucky one."

"Lucky? How can you say that?" she asked. "Your parents played favorites."

Antonio glanced at Isabella. She was curled up against the passenger side door with her arms crossed. If she was trying to keep her distance she was failing miserably. Isabella was already taking sides in his story.

"I was lucky because I wasn't pressured to perform better. My parents had high expectations for both of us, but I was lazy and unfocussed. Everyone knew that Gio was smarter, faster and better than me," he said matter-of-factly.

"That's not true," Isabella said.

"It was at the time," he said, frowning as he noticed how Isabella leapt to his defense. She'd used to do that when she read an unflattering news item about him, even when she didn't have all the facts. "Or it could have been my family's mindset. He was firstborn. He was the heir. Of course he was the best at everything."

"That is *so* unfair," she muttered. "I don't know how you could have stood it."

"Don't worry, it didn't last long," Antonio said. He glanced at Isabella as the streetlights flickered through the window. She looked upset for the child he'd used to be. "I hit my stride in my late teens."

"Uh-oh," she said. "You shook up the status quo?"

He nodded. "We started getting competitive. Gio needed a challenge, but he never thought I would eclipse him. I was tired of hearing, 'If only you were more like your brother…' I wanted someone to say that to Gio. And they did, but not in the way I wanted."

Isabella leaned closer. He caught a faint hint of her scent.

"What happened?"

Antonio shifted uncomfortably in his seat. "One day my father told us that he thought the Rossi empire was going to the wrong brother."

Isabella's gasp echoed in the car. "Why would he say that?"

"I think he said it to make Gio work harder. It made *me* work harder. I openly gloated, but I was secretly horrified." He hated how he had felt. How he had acted. Antonio closed his eyes, wishing he could forget the devastation in Gio's face. "For once I wasn't the other brother. The spare. And I wasn't going to have that taken away from me."

Isabella scooted closer. "But being the heir was part of Giovanni's identity?"

He nodded. "My father unintentionally created a

chasm between Gio and me. Our competition wasn't so friendly anymore. Gio saw me as a threat."

She reached over and placed her hand on his arm. "Did he hurt you?"

"No, there wasn't any physical fighting. And we were a team when we needed to be. But I learned to keep my thoughts private. I could never show what I wanted or what was important to me. Otherwise Gio would go after it."

"Like what?" Isabella asked.

He shrugged. "It was little things at first. I saved up and bought a motorcycle, but I didn't have it for more than a week before Gio stole it one night and wrecked it. Stuff like that."

"I don't consider that as *little* stuff," Isabella said. "He destroyed your property. It was vandalism. It was *wrong*. Why didn't your parents intervene?"

"At first they just believed that boys would be boys. Then they decided that it was a phase we would grow out of."

"It sounds like they just didn't want to take sides. Or deal with it," she said, and gave a sympathetic squeeze on his arm.

"Probably." He wanted to cover her hand with his and enjoy the feel of her. "Then it started to escalate. Sometimes I felt I was being paranoid. I had no proof he was behind the sabotage and the thefts, but I had my suspicions. And then we were in the running for the same honor at university. I knew he was going to pull something, but I didn't think he would get me expelled."

"He got you kicked out?" Isabella's voice trembled with outrage. "That's horrible. How did he do that?"

"He told the dean at the university that I was cheating and he manufactured evidence." His voice was calm and controlled, but cold anger weighed heavily against him as he remembered the injustice. No one had believed him. And to add insult to injury Gio had been commended for making the difficult decision to reveal the deceit of his own brother.

"Couldn't you have proved otherwise?" Isabella asked. "What about your parents? Didn't they defend you?"

He shrugged his shoulders, hiding the hurt. "My mother believed I was set up, but not by Gio." She had refused to hear a bad word about her firstborn, and Antonio still felt the sting of betrayal.

"And your father?"

The sting intensified. "He believed that I was cheating and that I had shamed the family," he said quietly. It was hard to get the words out. "I was disinherited."

"You were punished and Giovanni got away with it? Did you retaliate?"

"I wanted to, but my friends talked me out of it. They told me I was lucky to get out of that poisonous atmosphere and I needed to move on or it would destroy me. I knew they were right but I was still bitter."

"Something tells me that's an understatement," Isabella said. "Now I understand what drives you to work so hard."

It did have something to do with his success. He had something to prove. "Eventually my father welcomed me back into the family." He smiled as he remembered the awkward reconciliation. "After I made my first million. My father was very proud of what I had achieved without his help."

"And Giovanni never confessed?"

"No." He didn't know if Gio had kept silent because he'd wanted to enjoy the spoils of war or if he'd been afraid of what their disciplinarian father would have done if the truth came out. "I didn't speak to Gio for years. Not until I saw him at my father's funeral almost two years ago. He asked for forgiveness. It was sincere and genuine."

That was what his instincts had told him, but now he wondered if he had gotten it wrong. Maybe he'd wanted to believe Gio and have his brother back.

Isabella pulled her hand away from him. "And were you able to forgive?"

"Not forgive so much as move on," he admitted. "Gio should have felt secure. I didn't think we were in competition anymore. But for some reason I didn't trust that the treaty would last."

"He was your competitor for longer than he was your friend?"

Antonio nodded. That was why he'd he still been cautious around his brother. "I knew I had to keep my guard up. But I made a mistake." He paused, unsure if he wanted to reveal this to Isabella. "I couldn't hide how I felt about *you*." He felt Isabella's tension.

"So you think Giovanni went after me and I wasn't able to resist his charms? That's why you were so quick to believe him?"

"It fit his pattern. He went after something, or in this case someone, who was important to me."

Isabella leaned back in her seat. "Why didn't you tell me about this? You could have shared your concerns."

"I didn't think I had to." He had trusted Isabella, but he'd seen how close she'd become with Gio. He'd thought that Isabella wouldn't choose his brother over him. That she wasn't capable of crossing that line. But Gio's charm had been too seductive for her.

"It would have helped knowing that I was a target," Isabella said. "Or maybe you wanted to test me?"

"Why would I do that?" he asked, suddenly weary.

"Did you ever consider that your brother knew he could sabotage our relationship with just a lie? All he had to do was raise suspicion." She tossed her hands in the air. "He knew you wouldn't open up and talk about it. That your suspicion would fester until finally you couldn't trust me anymore."

"That's not what happened," Antonio said as anger curled inside him. Why was he telling her any of this? He should have kept quiet.

Isabella crossed her arms. "Your brother's ploy worked better than he could have imagined."

Antonio gritted his teeth. "You're giving Gio far more credit than he deserves."

"Giovanni played on the weakness in our relationship," she pointed out. "He was around enough to see what we couldn't. He knew you wouldn't talk about what was on your mind, and he knew I would do anything to get you back."

Isabella's words pricked at him. There was some truth in them. Hadn't he learned anything from the past?

"You kept making the same mistakes with your brother," Isabella accused. "But don't worry, Antonio. I've learned *my* lesson. We weren't meant to be together. I'm not fighting for us anymore."

Her words were like a punch to his chest. He wanted to say something sarcastic. Something biting. But it would only reveal how much he felt the loss. Instead Antonio stared straight ahead and pressed his foot harder on the gas pedal. Isabella might not like it when he went quiet, but he had learned that silence was his best shield.

CHAPTER NINE

ISABELLA lay in bed wide awake and restless. Her bed-sheet was tangled around her legs from her tossing and turning. The silence in Antonio's apartment made her tense. She stared at the ceiling, wondering if she had made the right decision to come back here. Lately she'd made the wrong choices. Like Giovanni.

When she had slept with Antonio's brother she had been drunk and deeply hurt. She blamed the alcohol, Giovanni—and herself. She didn't remember a lot about that night, but she knew she had made the choice. She could have stopped it anytime.

But she hadn't. Because she had been acting out. She had lost Antonio, allowed her dream to slip through her fingers, and she hadn't known why. She had tried to blunt the pain with drinking and partying. She'd sought comfort where she shouldn't have.

She couldn't change the past, but Isabella knew she wouldn't make those choices again. Next time she would recognize the warning signs of her own behavior. She'd have to; her baby was relying on her.

Isabella rubbed a protective hand over her stomach and heard a noise in the hallway. She lifted her head from the pillow and looked at the door. Her pulse skipped a beat when she saw a shadow underneath the door.

Antonio. He was coming to her. *Finally.*

She exhaled slowly as she stared at the strip of light underneath the door. She had been getting mixed signals from Antonio. He had refrained from touching her but she had felt his heated gaze. He had been the perfect gentleman but she sensed his self-control was barely contained.

Her restraint had been shaky, too. She wanted to be with him, but would it send her into a tailspin like last time? Did she want to be with him because she felt alone and scared of her future? Or did she want a do-over and nothing more?

Isabella watched the door as her heart pounded in her ears. Her chest was tight with anticipation. When she heard him mutter something softly in Italian and walk away, she bit her lip to prevent herself from calling out.

Antonio might want to relive the memories, but he obviously didn't think it was worth the risk. He still didn't trust her. Isabella sank back onto her pillow, disappointed.

She didn't trust her decision-making. What if she had invited him into her bed? Would it have taken her down the same path and brought the same outcome? Would she have regretted it?

No. She would regret not giving herself another chance.

"Antonio?"

Antonio felt his shoulders bunch when he heard Isabella's soft voice. He had tried to banish all thoughts of her by working, but his legendary focus was absent tonight. He needed to lose himself in reports and e-mails. It had almost worked. He hadn't heard Isabella enter his study. He didn't have a chance to put up his guard.

He glanced up from his laptop computer. His chest tightened when he saw her at the doorway. Her long blonde hair was tumbled, her face free of make-up. She wore only a white T-shirt and panties.

Isabella was a tantalizing mix of innocence and sin. Antonio clenched the edge of his desk, his fingers whitening as he struggled for control. The shirt barely skimmed the tops of her thighs. The thin cotton couldn't hide the shape of her breasts or the dark pink of her nipples. He didn't know why she bothered wearing it. It would take only a second to tear it off her body.

Don't do it. The words reverberated in Antonio's head as his gaze focused on her long, bare legs. His study was in the farthest corner of her apartment from the guestroom. It was his sanctuary and no one disturbed him when he was working. Antonio had thought he would be safe from temptation tonight. He hadn't thought she would seek him out.

"Yes?" he said, his voice hoarse.

She looped her long hair over her ear. "It's late."

It *was* late. Too late to stop what he had put into motion. When he'd asked her to stay for a few more days he had been looking for more than a shoulder to lean on. He needed Isabella to return to his side—and also to his bed. But when she had asked about the guestroom, he'd known she wasn't ready for them to become lovers again. After the way he'd treated her, the things he'd said, he couldn't blame her.

But it didn't stop him from hoping. Planning. Strategizing. He shouldn't consider getting her back. He should send Isabella away once and for all so he could focus on his responsibilities. Now that his brother had died Antonio needed to fix the mess Gio made of the family's fortune.

Yet all he could think about was Isabella.

"You shouldn't be working," she said as she leaned against the doorframe. The movement caused her T-shirt to hike up, offering him a glimpse of her tiny white panties.

He pulled his gaze away but it didn't stop the desire heating his blood. Antonio cleared his throat and pulled at the collar of his shirt. "I have a lot to do."

"Do you need any help?" Isabella offered.

He imagined Isabella assisting him. Leaning over his shoulder as her T-shirt gaped. Sitting primly on the edge of his desk, her legs brushing against him as she inadvertently offered a glimpse of white silk. Antonio swallowed back a groan as his imagination went wild. Isabella would be more distraction than help.

Distraction. That was putting it mildly. As he silently declined Isabella's offer with a shake of his head Antonio realized that Isabella had become an obsession. Thoughts of her interrupted his daily life. She invaded his dreams. He was addicted to her touch to the point that nothing else mattered.

This woman had destroyed him once. Yes, she had sent him soaring to the heavens, but she had also sent him crashing into hell. And he was willing to risk going through all that again if it meant one more night together.

What was it about this woman that made him so reckless? Was it how she had fit so perfectly in his arms? Was it her soft curves or the warmth of her smile?

No, it was more about how she had brightened his day. Just her presence had transformed his mausoleum of an apartment into a home.

But was that enough to make him forget that this woman had been unfaithful to him? That she'd cheated on him with his brother?

That reminder should have burned like acid, erasing any desire for her. He waited for dark emotions to wrap around him like a heavy cloak. But they didn't this time. He felt conflicted because he wasn't sure if she *had* cheated on him.

What is it about me that makes it so hard to believe?

"Excuse me?" Isabella frowned and pushed away from the doorframe.

Damn. He hadn't realized he had spoken out loud. "I was thinking about what you asked earlier. Why I have a difficult time believing you."

"You never gave me an answer." She crossed her arms and the cotton strained against her full breasts.

Antonio's mouth went dry. "I don't think I have one," he answered gruffly.

"You never asked me about my sexual past, but maybe that's because you didn't think you would like the answer."

He'd never asked because he didn't like the idea of her with another man. He had struggled with the unfamiliar possessiveness. Had he been willing to believe she was unfaithful because she was so incredibly sensual and eager? Had he assumed she was like that in bed with any man?

"I kind of have a reputation back home—but I didn't earn it," she said. "A lot of guys brag that I slept with them, but it isn't true."

It seemed Isabella was *always* struggling with her reputation. She was beautiful and sexy, and she wasn't cautious. The girls in her youth must have been jealous, but he also suspected that a few teenage boys had misread her friendly smile and bold attitude.

"I want you to know that I only had three boyfriends before I met you. And there was never any overlapping between. I also think you should know that I never had a one-night stand. I don't jump into bed with just anyone."

Three? That was it? Antonio was deeply grateful she didn't ask how many sexual partners *he* had had. He wasn't surprised that she had fallen into his bed the first day they'd met. They'd had an instantaneous connection and it had been so powerful she'd done something she wouldn't normally do.

"That day we met was special. Perfect," he said in a husky voice. "Too perfect."

"Too perfect?" She raised her eyebrows. "Is there such a thing?"

"Yes, because I always knew something that perfect couldn't last." He had often thought that Isabella had broken down his barriers, but now he realized that wasn't true. She had knocked some of them down, but he hadn't been as unguarded as he'd thought.

"It was supposed to be a fling," Isabella said. "It lasted longer than it should have because… Well, I held on longer than I should have." She looked away as she blushed. "I didn't mean to do that. I pushed too hard and I clung on tight when I should have let go."

"No, that's not true." When she'd pushed, he'd known she cared. When she had deferred her college education, he hadn't taken it for granted. He wasn't used to his loved ones choosing him first. It had felt strange and temporary. As if somehow he would mess it up and her loyalty would be taken away from him. That was why he had always been on his guard. "Maybe you should have pushed harder."

Isabella couldn't hide her surprise. "Are you kidding me?"

Antonio wasn't sure how to explain why he'd acted the way he had. He wasn't comfortable exposing this side of him. "We had a whirlwind affair. Everything was fast and furious."

"What's wrong with that?" she asked with a smile.

"I tried to shove a lifetime of memories into a few months, knowing it couldn't last." He frowned as he thought about what he had just said. "*Expecting* it wouldn't last."

"I don't understand," Isabella said, her smile fading. "*Why* couldn't it last? Did you *expect* me to cheat on you?"

"No, not exactly. I expected that it wouldn't take much for you to leave my side," he said. "I had nothing to hold you. You didn't want my money or enjoy high society. The sex was amazing, but I didn't think it was enough to keep you in my bed. For all I knew it was always like that for you."

"I was interested in *you*, Antonio," Isabella said. She looked stunned, with wide eyes and parted lips. "You were my world. I thought it was obvious. I would never have chosen your brother over you."

"But I didn't know that." He sighed and rubbed his face with his hands. Isabella had been faithful. He, however, hadn't shown any faith in her. "You were right: all Gio needed to do was plant a kernel of suspicion. I took care of the rest."

"Because you don't think anyone can be loyal to you. I understand that now." She rested her shoulder against the doorframe and sighed. "I wish I had known that a long time ago. I should have seen it."

"But you *were* loyal," he insisted. "You always took my side when you read the news or when my brother tried to rile me up. I noticed, but I didn't trust it. It was too good to be true. Even after all I did you didn't give up on me. You stayed here. You kept fighting for us."

But he had refused to see it that way. When she had remained in Rome with Gio he'd thought it was evidence of her infidelity. He had twisted her actions into proof that she'd betrayed him.

"Yeah," Isabella muttered, "that wasn't one of my better ideas."

Antonio barely heard her as he accepted he had been wrong. He'd allowed his insecurities to poison something beautiful. His actions sickened him. Isabella hadn't destroyed him. *He* had destroyed everything. He was his own worst enemy.

"I'm sorry, Isabella." His throat felt tight, but he had to get the words out. "What I put you through was unforgivable. None of this was your fault. I'm to blame."

She stared at him in surprise. It was obvious she'd never expected an apology and that shamed him even more.

Isabella nervously darted her tongue along her lips. "It's not *unforgivable*."

"I don't deserve your forgiveness. Your kindness," he said slowly. "Even now, after all I've said and done, after I promised you a ticket back to Los Angeles, you're still here. Simply because I asked."

"Well…" She nervously pressed her hand against her

chest and cleared her throat. "My motivations aren't *that* pure."

Antonio heard the sensual promise in her voice and his heartbeat began to gallop. His gaze slowly traveled from her eyes to her feet. "So I gather."

Isabella didn't know what she was doing. No, that wasn't quite true. She had plans to seduce Antonio. She had done it dozens of time before without second-guessing herself. But this time she wasn't sure. Would he reject her out of guilt? Bed her and then have a change of heart once the sun came up? He'd asked for forgiveness, but would he cruelly kick her out of his bed again?

His reaction could be even worse. What would Antonio think of her if she propositioned him? She had told him the truth about her sexual past, but did he believe her? Her brazen act could blow up in her face. He could twist it around and believe that her passionate nature couldn't be contained. That she wanted a man—any man. He might even believe that she'd seduced Giovanni in the same manner.

That thought made her want to run back to the safety of her room. But she didn't want to play it safe anymore. She didn't want to stand on the sidelines and wait for permission. She wanted to live again. Love. Be with Antonio once more.

She took a step forward. Her legs shook, but there was no way she could hide it. Isabella knew she should have worn something different. She wished she had sexy lingerie or something more feminine. She shouldn't attempt to seduce someone as sophisticated as Antonio wearing an oversized T-shirt. In the past it hadn't mattered what she wore, but then she had been confident of the outcome. This time she needed all the help she could get.

She shouldn't even attempt this, she decided as she took another step forward, but she knew she hadn't been bold since the moment Antonio had kicked her out of his bed. She had lost everything that was important to her and become too afraid to make a move. Those days were over. She wanted to be her old self again.

Antonio closed his laptop computer, his eyes never leaving hers. He rose from his chair and walked around his desk. He was silent and his movements were deliberate, reminding her of a hunter circling his prey.

Isabella's stomach clenched as her gaze traveled down the length of him. Antonio Rossi was effortlessly sexy. His shirt accentuated his broad shoulders and muscular arms. She shivered as she remembered what it was like to be held in his embrace.

She had always felt safe and secure when she was in his arms. She could go wild with lust and still know Antonio would take care of her. He would take to the heights of ecstasy and hold her when she felt like she would shatter into pieces. And then he would curl her against his chest and hold her all night long.

Desire, thick and overpowering, coiled tight in her belly as her gaze traveled from his flat stomach to the dark jeans that emphasized his powerful legs. She noticed his bare feet and her mouth twitched into a small smile. She always liked it when he was casual and barefoot. It didn't make him any less intimidating. Instead it stripped away another layer of civility and gave her a glimpse of the earthy man underneath.

Isabella slowly raised her gaze back to his face. Her skin went hot when she saw the lust in his dark eyes.

She didn't have to worry whether or not her seduction was going to work. He was going to take her to bed before she could make a move. He was going to make love to her. Hard, fast and wild.

She could barely catch her breath as the excitement pressed against her chest. Antonio would make love to every inch of her. She shook with anticipation and her knees threatened to collapse.

The baby.

Isabella lowered her gaze, shielding her thoughts from Antonio. What would he think about the gradual changes in her body? Her breasts already seemed larger and more sensitive. Her belly wasn't as flat as it used to be. And what if she woke up in his bed and had morning sickness? That would permanently ruin the mood.

Maybe she was taking too much of a risk. She should back down. Accept that what they had was truly over. Run away. Go back to her room and lock the door.

Isabella hated that idea. Her feet refused to move. She didn't want to give up Antonio. It was time to reclaim him and the woman she'd used to be. It was time to be bold and grab her dreams before they got away from her.

She wanted this. She raised her lashes and looked directly in his eyes. She wanted Antonio. She would regret not having this one last time with him. She couldn't get back what they'd used to have, but she could end this relationship with a happy memory.

"I need to know something first," Isabella said in a rush as emotions swirled around her so fast that she could barely speak. What she was about to ask could ruin the moment, but she needed to know. "Do you trust me?"

"Yes."

He didn't hesitate or embellish. She saw the certainty in his eyes. One little word and he had given her something she'd never thought she'd have again. He trusted her.

That was all she needed to know.

CHAPTER TEN

ISABELLA had longed for Antonio for months. His touch had haunted her and she knew she would never have the same experience with another man. She trembled before him, eager to touch him again—but what if they couldn't recapture the magic? What if everything that has happened between them cast a dark shadow and she could never reach that pinnacle of beauty and love again?

Their gazes clashed and Isabella felt the anticipation stirring deep inside her. From the look in his eyes, Antonio had no qualms. He knew what he wanted and he wasn't going to wait anymore.

Isabella's gasp was muffled as he claimed her mouth with his. He demanded entry and she kissed him hungrily, matching his aggression. She couldn't fight her shameful response to his forceful nature.

He bunched her cotton T-shirt in his hands. Isabella wanted him to wrench it from her body. Tear it off. She felt the tremor in his fingers as he peeled the shirt over her breasts and shoulders. When he pulled it over her head and tossed it on the floor Isabella knew he was trying to slow down. Hold back. He didn't want to scare her with the intensity he felt. Didn't he realize that she felt the same?

Antonio gathered her close against him. She sighed when he wrapped his arms around her. His shirt rasped her tight nipples and she moaned against his mouth. His hands slid down her body as he roughly caressed her curves. He impatiently shoved her panties down her legs. When she kicked them aside, he grabbed her waist and pressed her against his erection.

Isabella felt her desire heat and thicken as it flared low in her pelvis. She knew this was going to be fast and furious. She already felt out of control. Her world tilted and she grabbed onto Antonio's shirt.

She felt Antonio lower her onto the floor. Their kisses grew untamed. She pulled him closer as he knelt between her legs. Isabella felt surrounded by Antonio as she inhaled his scent and felt masculine heat coming off him in waves. All she could see and feel was him, but it wasn't enough. She needed him closer. She needed him deep inside her.

Isabella jerked her mouth away, her lips swollen, her lungs burning for air. She grabbed the back of his head, clutching at his dark, thick hair as he licked trail down her neck.

His hands were everywhere and she offered no resistance. He knew what she liked. Antonio remembered her pleasure points, teasing and stroking her until she didn't think she could take it anymore. Antonio's touch was merciless as he wrung out every bit of pleasure.

Her defenses were crumbling. She couldn't wait, and the forbidden thrill chased through her blood. She wanted to see Antonio in his conquering glory. She wanted him to claim her heart and soul.

As Antonio drew her nipple deep in his mouth he boldly cupped her mound with his hand. She bucked against his possessive touch, moaning as Antonio dipped his fingers into her moist heat.

Isabella stretched her arms on the floor in surrender. She was his for the taking. He gently massaged her sex, teasing her as he kissed along her hipbone. She bucked her hips restlessly. She thought she was going to go out of her mind with wanting.

"More." Her breaths came out in short pants. She wanted it all, and she wanted it right now, because she didn't think she'd get another chance.

Antonio didn't respond, but she knew he wouldn't deny her. She could ask for anything and he'd give it to her. He always fulfilled her deepest needs. He parted her legs wider with a forceful hand and lowered his mouth against her sex. Isabella cried out in ecstasy at the first flick of his tongue.

His touch was just as addictive as she remembered. Antonio swiftly took her to the edge and then held back. She begged for his touch, pleaded for satisfaction as he took her pleasure to another level. Just when she thought her mind would shatter, Antonio granted her the sexual release she craved. He ruthlessly drove her over the edge and a white-hot climax consumed her.

She was shaking with the aftershocks when she heard the rustle of his clothes and felt the tip of his penis pressing against the entrance to her core. Isabella groaned when he gave a savage thrust. She tilted her hips to accommodate his heavy thickness and curled her fingers into his shoulders, digging her nails into his shirt.

Antonio withdrew almost completely. Isabella cried out as her core clenched. She then saw the look on

Antonio's face. His features were blunted with lust and his eyes glittered with need.

"I can never get enough of you," he growled as he plunged into her.

His thrusts were long and measured. It was testament to his willpower. But as Isabella went wild underneath him his relentless rhythm broke free. He grabbed her hips, his fingers digging into her skin, and sank deep into her heat. He tensed and shuddered as she let out a hoarse cry of triumph.

He collapsed onto her. Isabella wrapped her arms around him as his choppy breath warmed the crook of her neck. Antonio didn't say anything as they tried to catch their breath. She felt small tremors rocking her heated body as Antonio raised his head.

"Don't fall asleep on me now, Bella." He looked down at her face, his eyes gleaming with sensual promise as he picked her up and carried her out of the room. "The night has just begun.

Isabella gasped and her eyes widened as she escaped from a bad dream. She jackknifed into a sitting position and looked around, ready to escape. Her heart was racing. She was shivering but her skin felt hot and sweaty.

It took her a few moments before she recognized her surroundings. It was turning dawn. In Rome, she noticed as she glanced through the window. She was in Antonio's bedroom. Not Giovanni's.

She was with Antonio. Isabella studied him in the shadowy room as he lay sleeping. He was sprawled across the bed, naked and glorious. She wasn't reliving that horrible moment three months ago. It was just a bad dream mixed with a bad memory.

Isabella instinctively reached for Antonio to rouse him. She needed to be in his strong arms. There she would feel safe and secure. Her fingers slowly curled against his shoulders and she stopped herself.

What was she thinking? She couldn't tell Antonio about her bad dream. She couldn't discuss Giovanni. Not while they were sharing a bed. Not when they just had made love. Antonio would think she was comparing him with his brother.

Isabella pressed her hand against her head. She felt a little dizzy from moving so fast. She lowered herself carefully, gently resting her head on the pillow, and faced Antonio.

When would she stop having these dreams? Isabella cautiously closed her eyes, hoping she didn't fall into a troubled sleep again. She had heard that pregnant women often had strange dreams and nightmares. Something about worry and hormones colliding. Isabella really hoped that wasn't the case. She didn't think she could take another six months of this.

Isabella stilled when Antonio shifted. His arm draped over her side and he nestled her against his chest. She pressed her lips together as she resisted temptation to melt against him. As Antonio cradled her his large hand spanned her abdomen.

Her breath caught in her lungs as the protective gesture nearly undid her. Even in his sleep he was fulfilling his promise. He would look after this baby. Emotions stung her eyes and clogged her throat. She didn't move and she kept her eyes closed.

Had he noticed the changes in her body? She didn't think he had. Throughout the night he had shown his appreciation for her body. He had been fascinated and had paid particular attention to her breasts. Isabella blushed at the erotic memories. From what she remembered, he'd made no mention of any changes.

She waited for Antonio to move his hand. Nothing happened. He continued to sleep soundly as she rested her head against his bare chest. His warm breath wafted over her skin and his broad chest rubbed against her back. Isabella slowly exhaled, but the tension didn't leave her body.

Isabella reached for Antonio's hand and carefully removed it from her stomach. She couldn't let him get this close. She couldn't get used to this. She had already taken too many risks. All for the sake of being with Antonio one more time.

It had been worth it, but she couldn't indulge in this kind of recklessness. The child was reality and Antonio was fantasy. She needed to remember that.

She didn't want to hide anything from Antonio, but she had to protect herself. She wasn't going to look for emotional support from him only to feel the sharp sting of rejection. It was only a matter of time before Antonio would move on and find a suitable woman. A society wife. She needed to rely on *her* strength and not his when that happened.

Isabella squeezed her eyes shut as tears burned. She took a choppy breath and slowly turned around, her back facing Antonio. She wanted to talk through her fears about being pregnant and share her dreams for her child. But she couldn't. She had to go through this alone.

She needed to start making plans. Although she had only promised a few days, Isabella knew she was taking a step back. If she weren't careful she would promise a few more days, and then a few weeks. She wouldn't find the strength to break away. She'd be clinging onto this relationship again.

It was time to create some distance. Isabella slowly moved from Antonio's embrace. She suddenly felt cold. She wanted to return to Antonio's bed and curl up against him.

It was tempting. Isabella wavered for a moment, and was about to lie back down when she felt a wave of nausea. It was a sign of morning sickness she couldn't ignore. Pressing her hand against her mouth, Isabella hurried back to her room.

Antonio stretched his tired muscles as a satisfied growl rumbled in his chest. He finally had Isabella back in his bed. All was right with the world, he thought with a lazy smile. He reached for Isabella, wanting to hold her against him and enjoy the feel of her warm skin against his.

His hand touched the bedsheet. Antonio blinked and opened his eyes. Isabella wasn't there. The pillow still held an indentation, but the wrinkled sheets were cool. She had slipped out of his bed hours ago.

What the hell was going on here? Antonio jumped out of bed, his feet hitting the floor as he strode to the door. Isabella had never left him while he slept. If she didn't wake him up with the sweetest kisses and caresses, he was the one to wake *her*, in the most wickedly erotic ways. He was getting hard just remembering.

He reached the guestroom in record time and opened the door without knocking. Isabella was curled up in her bed, sound asleep. "Bella?"

She raised her head with a start. Her hair was still damp from a shower and a bathtowel was wrapped around her. "Oh, I lay down and fell asleep again," she said groggily. "What time is it?"

"Why are you sleeping here?" he asked as he towered over her. "Why did you leave my bed?"

"Uh, because I wanted to get some rest." Her eyes widened as her gaze traveled down his naked body. He saw the flare of desire in her eyes and couldn't hide his response.

But it didn't change a very important fact. She'd had sex with him and then she had left. That wasn't like Isabella. She'd used to burrow as close as she could and cling to him throughout the night. Now she couldn't get away fast enough. "Bella, do you see me as a one-night stand?"

"Um…" She shoved her tangled hair from her face.

"You just wanted one more time before you left? Needed to scratch an itch and nothing more?" He wouldn't allow it. When they'd been together it had been wild and mind-blowing because there had been no games or limits. Just pure sensation and emotion.

"What if it was?" she asked with a hint of defiance.

He was no one-night stand or meaningless fling. Antonio wanted to be the most important person in her life. He was used to being second choice, but not with her. He wanted their past and their future to be inextricably linked. He was prepared to bind her to him in any way possible.

"Then I will change your mind," he said, and he flipped the bedsheet over and crawled into her bed.

CHAPTER ELEVEN

Isabella tightly held the edges of the towel as she scooted to the edge of the mattress. "Antonio, don't pretend that this is anything more than what it is."

He slid his hands underneath her and pulled her close to him. She wanted to push him away but that would mean losing the towel.

"Why did you leave our bed?" he asked.

His tone was firm and it held a dangerous edge that made her hot.

"Your bed," she corrected him. They didn't share anything. Not anymore. It would be good to remember that.

"*Our* bed."

No, it had never been theirs. It was his bed, his apartment, his world. She was a temporary guest. She didn't belong here and probably never had.

"Really? Our bed?" she asked. She struggled to hold her towel in place as he placed a kiss against her collarbone. She felt his smile against her quickened pulse. "How many women have slept there since I've been gone?"

He lifted his head and held her gaze. "Don't even

try," he warned softly. "I know you want to create a barrier between us. I won't let you."

Isabella gritted her teeth. He had no right. She needed to place a short expiration date on this relationship. If she could even call it that. This time she couldn't get caught up in a whirlwind affair. She needed a stable environment for her baby.

She would love to think that they could try again and their affair would last longer. But who was she kidding? Would he want her when she was heavy with child? How long would it be before he needed to marry and have children of his own? She didn't fit any of the requirements he had for a wife and there was no getting around that.

"I left because it's not our bed anymore," she said. "We are no longer a couple."

"We have a connection that can't be broken." He threaded his hands through her hair and spread it across her pillow.

She winced when his fingers got tangled in her hair. "That doesn't make us a couple."

Antonio smoothed his fingertips along the side of her face before cupping her jaw with his strong hand. He tilted her face so she couldn't look away from his serious gaze. "Why do you think I asked you to stay?"

"For the sex." She knew that was the truth. He couldn't argue with that.

"And that's all?" he asked lightly as his hand drifted down her throat to her chest.

Her skin tingled from his touch and she was having difficulty remembering what they were talking about. She should get out of this bed and into some clothes, but she couldn't move. She didn't want to.

"When we're together you have the ability to shut out the world," she said. They both did. Time stood still when they were making love. "You want to do that because you're dealing with a family crisis. That's why you want me around. So you can take me to your bed and lose yourself."

"I want to make love to you," he admitted. His fingers dipped behind her towel.

Isabella's chest rose and fell as she felt his fingers graze her breasts.

"But I also want more from you."

She swiped her tongue along her bottom lip "More?"

"I need you at my side," he confessed in a low, husky voice. "When you're there, I feel like I can conquer the world."

Isabella wanted to believe she had that kind of influence in Antonio's life, but she knew it wasn't true. She was an ordinary girl with no special skills or powers. "You don't rely on anyone, Antonio."

"It may not look like it, but I do," he said as he gently tugged the towel from her slackened grasp. "It meant a lot to me when I could wake up and see you in my bed. When you shared how you felt and what you thought. When you changed the course of your life to be with me."

"That was then." She couldn't make those sacrifices again.

"But you're still looking after me," he pointed out as he parted the towel and revealed her body to him. Her nipples puckered and his eyes darkened with pleasure. "You delayed your trip back to Los Angeles to be with me. You had no trouble sharing your feelings and thoughts, even though I might disagree. But when I woke up you weren't in my bed."

He hadn't noticed. He didn't realize that she was having trouble sharing her fears and dreams. She wasn't going to tell him. This time she was holding back. She wasn't giving him everything because she didn't want to get hurt again.

"Your bed?" she teased, determined to distract him from the truth. Let him think she was the same as before. It was only for a few days. "I thought it was *our* bed."

Antonio wrapped his hands around her wrists and lifted her arms above her head. She twisted her body in protest, her skin tingling as she thrust out her chest.

"Stay next time," he ordered softly.

"I can't promise you that." She wanted to bite her tongue. She should have just agreed. He wasn't going to let this go until he got his way.

"There was a time when you never wanted to leave my bed," Antonio said as he dipped his head and took her tight nipple in his mouth.

Pleasure, white-hot and blinding, crackled through her body. "Antonio!" she exclaimed. She tried to pull away, but he held onto her wrists. She arched against him, trying to get closer.

When he turned his attention to her other breast his touch was just as ruthless as he took her almost to the height of ecstasy. Just when she thought she would shatter he pulled back, denying her release.

"Please, Antonio," she said in between gasps as hot pleasure pressed just under her skin. "Let go of me. I want to touch you."

Antonio raised his head and she saw the glitter in

his eyes. He bestowed upon her a hard, almost brutal kiss before he let go her wrists. She greedily clasped her hands on the back of his head and pressed his mouth on her breast.

He teased her nipple with the edge of his teeth and grabbed her hips. Her fractured sigh echoed in the quiet room as he urgently caressed her body.

Antonio pulled away and gazed down at her. His features were carved and taut with desire. "So beautiful," he murmured as though he were mesmerized.

He surged forward, capturing her mouth with his, and gently parted her legs with his hands. Antonio pressed his hand against the apex of her thighs and growled his appreciation. She was so aroused that she couldn't hide it even if she wanted to.

Antonio plunged his tongue into her mouth and caressed her swollen clitoris. Isabella rocked against his hand as she chased the pleasure coiling low in her pelvis. The sensations were so exquisite that it almost hurt.

"Now, Antonio," she said against his mouth. "Take me now."

She reached for him, but Antonio ignored her hands. His face was grim as he grasped her waist. He lifted her hips slightly and nestled his erection at the juncture of her thighs.

Isabella felt the rounded tip of his penis prodding against her. She wrapped her legs around his waist and held on tight. She took a deep breath just as he slowly penetrated her.

Isabella closed her eyes and bit her bottom lip as he stretched and filled her to the hilt. Antonio paused and she felt his muscles twitch as he fought for self-control. His fingers trembled as they dug into her hips.

Antonio retreated and gave a deep thrust. Her pulse skipped a beat and her breath hitched in her throat as pleasure tightened inside her, ready to spring wildly and explode. He bucked against her and sensations showered through her like fireworks.

Antonio withdrew slightly before driving into her wet heat. Isabella gasped and dug her nails in his shoulders. One more deep thrust and she knew she would climax hard. She would need Antonio to hold her tight as she splintered into pieces.

He gave a shallow thrust.

"More," she whispered urgently. But Antonio didn't move. He held her tightly, his muscles shuddering as his restraint started to slip.

She opened her eyes and his gaze ensnared hers. The stark need in the dark depths was raw and elemental. More powerful than she'd ever seen.

"First," he said in a gravelly voice, "tell me why you won't share my bed."

Her eyelashes fluttered as she tried to hide her eyes. Why wouldn't he let the matter drop? Why did he find it so significant? "What did you say?" she asked as she frantically tried to come up with a believable excuse.

"I can take you against the window." He rocked against her tauntingly, reminding her of the pleasures he could give her. "Or on the floor. But you won't stay in my bed?"

She shook her head, refusing to meet his eyes that willed her to answer. Need pulsed inside her. "It's not important."

"I disagree. I think it's very important." Determination rang clearly in his raspy voice.

"Please, Antonio." She desperately bucked her hips, hoping his willpower would give away. "Don't stop."

Tension rolled through him, but Antonio didn't move. "That's up to you."

"I don't have a reason," she said on a sob. She was shaking and her body burned for satisfaction. He couldn't be this cruel.

"It's because you don't trust me like you used to." He reached down to where they were intimately joined and pressed his thumb on her clitoris. She shuddered, gasping for air as white-hot pleasure streaked through her. "I'm not going to kick you out of my bed again. I promise."

"You can't give me that kind of guarantee," she said between gasps. Was that why she'd had the bad dream? Because he had kicked her out of bed once before and knew he could do it again? She couldn't think straight, was tempted to tell him anything he wanted to know. Her body demanded release.

"Bella," his voice was thick and uneven. "Promise me—"

"Yes! Yes!" she cried out recklessly. "I'll share your bed."

She was rewarded with a series of deep, plunging thrusts. Her body accepted each stroke with unrestrained hunger. She writhed against Antonio, her movements frantic. His unforgiving rhythm made her delirious. Her breath snagged in her chest and a hush blanketed her mind as a violent climax lashed through her.

Her core clenched and squeezed Antonio. His muscles rippled with a hard tremor and his thrusts were suddenly wild and untamed. Antonio tilted his head back, his eyes shut, the tendons of his neck straining, as he unwillingly surrendered to the demands of his body. His hoarse cry tore at her heart and he gave one final, powerful thrust before tumbling on top of her.

As she clung to Antonio, Isabella tiredly stroked his sweat-slickened back. She didn't know if she'd made the right decision. She'd always thought that she learned from her mistakes, but she was right back where she had started. Only this time she wasn't so naïve. Not that it would help. She was still hopelessly in love with Antonio.

If only she had more willpower. She shouldn't have made that promise.

She didn't protest when Antonio rolled on his back and gathered her in his arms. She relaxed as she listened to his strong heartbeat. It felt right being with him. She should enjoy it while it lasted. What could possibly happen in two more days?

"The other bed is so much better," he said.

Was he wondering if she would follow through on the promise she'd made in the heat of the moment? "I agree. Much more room."

"You should move your things into the master bedroom," he said as he stroked her back with his strong fingers. "No point in keeping them here."

He wasn't giving her any room to retreat and hide. Antonio was making it clear that they were going to resume where they'd left off.

"I'm only going to be here for two more days. It's not worth the effort."

His fingers went still against her spine. "Two days?"

No, no, no. She recognized his tone but was not ready

to renegotiate. "Antonio, I'm not staying here any longer. We agreed."

Antonio rolled over and braced his arms on either side of her. His abdomen rested lightly against hers as he settled his hips between her thighs. He surrounded her, and she hated how her body softened and yielded to his.

"About that…" he drawled.

CHAPTER TWELVE

ANTONIO entered his apartment and heard Isabella's laughter coming from another room. He imagined the way she would toss back her head and her blonde hair would cascade over her shoulder. She put her whole body into it. It was always a beautiful sight and he couldn't get enough of it. He did everything he could to keep her laughing.

He paused at the threshold and allowed the joy of his home to wash over him after a stressful day. The music that blared from Isabella's MP3 player was fun, vibrant and very American. It should be at odds with his apartment's décor, but he liked it. It reminded him of Isabella.

Antonio closed the heavy front door and heard Isabella's footsteps. She rounded the corner with her usual exuberant style and Antonio stilled at the sight of her. Her hair was pulled back into a high ponytail and she wore one of his sweaters. It was too big, but the colour brought out the blue in her eyes. The sleeves were folded up and the hem went to her knees. It also concealed her curves. He liked seeing her in his clothes and in his home, but he wanted to see more of her. *All* of her.

His gaze traveled down and he gave an appreciative

whistle when he saw her legs encased in form-fitting black leggings. "I see you went shopping."

"I did," Isabella said as she draped her arms over his shoulders and leaned into him.

His hand automatically rested on the small of her back and he drew her close. He took a moment to savor her softness and warmth as she kissed him.

Antonio deepened the kiss and she matched his eagerness. They hadn't seen each other all day and all he wanted to do was take her to bed, shut out the world and reacquaint himself with Isabella's body.

But he couldn't do that anymore, Antonio reminded himself and reluctantly pulled away. He'd promised he wouldn't be selfish and isolate Isabella. He had been good on his word for the past month. Antonio had introduced her to his friends and important business associates. It had been a pleasant surprise to discover that not only was Isabella a natural hostess, but that she had already become close with his friends.

"What did you do today?" Antonio asked as he smoothed his hand along the curve of her hip.

"Fia came over for lunch and she took me to some great shops. I needed a couple of things to replace my old clothes. What do you think?" She raised her arms and spun around.

Antonio saw how his sweater draped over her stomach. His heart skipped a beat as he noticed the small bump.

Giovanni's baby.

He had dreaded this moment because he'd been unable to predict how he would respond. Isabella was now noticeably pregnant with his brother's child.

"Well?" Isabella asked warily.

He took a step forward and placed his palm gently over her stomach. His large hand rested perfectly against the baby bump. "You look beautiful."

She blushed and dipped her head. "Are you sure?"

Her shyness surprised him. It wasn't like her. He suddenly understood Isabella's concern. Did she think she would be less attractive to him? Or that the baby would be a constant reminder of her one night with his brother?

He didn't know how to reassure her. The baby wouldn't come between them. It would bind them closer together. Antonio was about to remove his hand but Isabella placed hers over his fingers. He held her gaze but she didn't say anything.

She didn't have to. At this moment nothing else existed. They were sharing this journey as parents together.

"I can't wait to meet this baby," he confessed. "She's going to look just like you."

"That would be unfortunate if 'she' turns out to be a boy."

Antonio watched her smile and his heart did a slow tumble. He loved Isabella. Deeply, madly and irrevocably. He wanted to be with her forever—and not because of the baby or the terms of Gio's will. He wanted to share every moment with her, starting now.

Antonio must have had an intense look. Isabella frowned and took a step back. "I shouldn't have stolen your sweater, but it's so soft and cozy."

"What's mine is yours," Antonio said, and he meant it.

Isabella's eyelashes flickered with uncertainty. Was

she uncomfortable because she didn't think she had anything to give *him*?

Then she was wrong. Isabella had made his apartment a home once again. The music, color and laughter seemed brighter this time around. His life had been stagnant and bitter after she had gone. Lonely. Now he felt surrounded by her love.

Isabella chuckled nervously and pulled at the collar of the sweater. "That's very generous of you, but I'll start with the sweater."

"You need to think bigger," he encouraged. "It's time to make some changes around here."

He looked around the apartment and saw the small additions Isabella had made. The big bouquet of yellow and orange flowers made him think of her bold personality. A small picture frame held a photo of the two of them when they'd visited the Trevi Fountain late one night. A bright red throw was casually draped on a chair and he imagined Isabella there moments ago, curled up and waiting for him.

He also noticed something else. This apartment wasn't ready for a child. "We need to baby-proof this place. And turn the guestroom into a nursery. Don't worry about the cost," he said when he saw Isabella's eyes widen. "Only the best for this baby."

Isabella knew her mouth was hanging open as she stared at Antonio. Had he just said the word *nursery*?

"You…you want to do what?"

"We haven't done anything to prepare for the baby," Antonio said as he curled his arm around her shoulder.

"There's no need to worry about that," she said as she

looked around the room. She couldn't imagine a child growing up here. *Her* child. "I've got plenty of time."

Antonio's hand tensed at her choice of pronoun. "The baby arrives in four months."

"No, that's not right. The due date is in late March."

"Right. Four months," he repeated patiently. "It's already November."

Oh, my God. Isabella went rigid as she recalled the date. How had that happened? She had been staying at Antonio's for more than a month. She'd only been supposed to stay for a few days and then Antonio had suggested she extend it for a weekend. And then another week. After a while she'd stopped asking about the plane ticket. But she couldn't believe over a month had already passed.

She was enjoying her stay with Antonio. It was better than anything she had hoped for. In some ways she felt their relationship was much stronger than when she'd first met him. She knew him better and had had a glimpse of his world. She also believed that he would be there for her when she needed him.

But it was time for her to go. What had started out as a vacation fling had derailed her from her goals. And, as much as she hated to think about it, she was keeping Antonio from what he needed. One day he would have to find a suitable wife.

"Antonio, I would enjoy tackling that project, but I'm not going to stay here for much longer. In fact, I think I should leave by the end of the week."

"I don't understand," Antonio said with a fierce frown. "I thought you were happy here?"

"I am," she quickly assured him. "These have been the happiest days of my life. But I've taken a huge detour from my future plans and it's time for me to return home."

"Is this about returning to college?" he asked. "Because you don't need a degree. I can take care you and the baby. I want to."

But she didn't want to be a kept woman. She needed to stand on her own two feet and take full responsibility for her child. "I made a promise to my mom. And, actually, it was also a promise to myself. I have to do this."

Antonio sighed. "I can't talk you out of it, can I?"

He could. That was part of the problem. She hugged him tightly and rested her head against his shoulder. "I'm going to miss you."

"I want you to visit Rome during your next Spring Break."

"I can't travel that late in my pregnancy." And she was worried that if she returned to Rome she would be reminded of everything she'd given up and wouldn't finish her college education.

"Then I will visit Los Angeles and be there for the birth," he promised.

"Sure." But she wouldn't hold him to his promise. He led a busy life that offered a great deal more than she could. She wasn't naïve. Long-distance relationships didn't work with someone like Antonio. Once she left Rome she would be out of sight and out of mind.

"I mean it, Bella. Whenever you need me, I'll be there."

CHAPTER THIRTEEN

TODAY was her last day with Antonio.

It hadn't quite sunk in, Isabella thought as she lay in bed watching the sunrise over Rome. She wanted to create some lasting memories. She wanted to remember Antonio's passion and heat. She needed to touch and taste him one last time. It was her wish to end the relationship on a kiss and then she could say goodbye.

Isabella reached out and cupped Antonio's jaw. The dark stubble was rough against her soft palm. She stroked the sharp angles and hard planes of his face, remembering the lines fanning his eyes when he smiled and the grooves bracketing his mouth when he frowned. She was going to miss his scowls as much as his sexy, slow smiles.

She lowered her head and brushed her lips against his. Isabella didn't know how she was going to live without Antonio's kisses again. Whenever he claimed her mouth with gentle seduction, or with hot, pulsing need, it was like an electric current snaked through her veins. She felt wildly alive each time Antonio touched her.

Isabella lips grazed Antonio's mouth again and she felt his body shift. "Bella..." he said in a sleepy growl.

Her breath hitched in her throat as a bittersweet ache filled her chest. She loved the way he said her name. It was a mix of masculine satisfaction and adoration. She hoped that it would always be that way when he thought of her.

Isabella trailed her hand down the thick column of his neck and memorized the strong lines and bronze skin. She gave a start when Antonio draped his arm around her waist and his fingers spanned her side. She felt the possessiveness in his touch through her T-shirt.

She glanced up at his face and her gaze collided with his. The sleep faded from his eyes and he studied her face with serious intent.

Isabella lowered her lashes, veiling her eyes from him. She didn't want him to read her thoughts. Her sadness.

Her hand stilled against his chest as Antonio bunched her T-shirt in his fist. "Why," he asked softly, "do you hide underneath this when you know I want you naked in bed?"

She smiled at the teasing quality in his voice. "I wear it so you will have the pleasure of taking it off me." That was partly true. What she didn't add was that she wore an oversized T-shirt to conceal her baby bump.

"No, you do it because you want to tease me." He let go of the cotton and tucked both his hands under his head. "This time I want *you* to take it off."

A wicked curl of excitement unfurled low in her pelvis. Antonio didn't simply want her to strip for him. He wanted her to express how she was feeling—or rather how he made her feel.

Isabella knelt beside Antonio on the mattress, her gaze never leaving his. She reached for the hem of her shirt. Her fingers flexed against the cotton. Today she wouldn't hold back.

She slowly raised the shirt, sensuously rolling her hips and arching her spine as anticipation sizzled in her veins. She felt Antonio's hot gaze on her skin. It made her feel scandalous and beautiful. She wasn't worried about her pregnant belly. Isabella thrust her breasts out and stretched as she freed herself of the shirt.

Antonio didn't move but watched in intense silence as she tossed the shirt onto the floor. She was naked before him. Instead of feeling shy, she felt gloriously alive.

Heat suffused her skin as she caressed her collarbone and shoulders. He was unnaturally still as he watched her. His harsh features and radiating tension were subtle responses. She didn't want that. She wanted to shatter that self-control once and for all.

Isabella massaged the tips of her breasts just like Antonio would. She bit her lip and moaned as her nipples stung. Antonio's chest rose and fell as he watched her hands trail down her body. Isabella felt like a harem girl pleasing her master. She felt powerful but submissive. Daring yet obedient. She wanted to give Antonio his fantasy, but at the same time she wanted to make him beg.

She skimmed her fingers along her pelvic bone. Just when she was about to cup her sex with her hand she changed her mind. She grasped Antonio's hard erection that angled toward his flat stomach. Antonio gasped, his hips vaulting off the mattress as she curled his fingers around his thickness.

Isabella pumped her hand with slow deliberation. She watched Antonio's eyes squeeze shut as his mouth slackened. His big hands clenched the pillow under his head. She was fascinated as she watched pleasure and agony chase across his face.

She bent down and wrapped her lips around the tip of his penis. Antonio's jagged breath was the sweetest sound to her ears. She sighed with delight as his large hands knotted in her hair. His fingers twisted with every swirl of her tongue and the deep draw of her mouth.

Isabella felt the tremors storm through his hard body and heard his uneven breath. He was so close to surrendering to her. She felt his hands dig into her shoulders as he urgently dragged her up his body.

She gave a cry of complaint. As much as she wanted to lie with him naked, she was determined to give him everything he desired. She wished she was bold enough to show him, tell him how she felt.

Driven by an urgency that scared her, Isabella pressed her mouth against Antonio's ear. Her heart was pounding against her ribcage and her nerves tingled just under her skin.

"I love you," she whispered.

Antonio didn't move. Isabella's heart lurched and plummeted. At that moment she felt more exposed than when she had stripped off her clothes. She was glad she'd had the courage to finally tell Antonio, and she refused to regret her impulsive words, but she didn't dare look at him.

She flinched when he cradled her jaw with unsteady hands. She kept her gaze lowered, not willing to see if there was rejection or indifference in his eyes. She was unprepared when Antonio covered her mouth with his. The kiss was raw and untamed. Isabella felt weak as the heat rushed in her blood.

Antonio's hands were everywhere, drawing her

closer, molding her body against his. She wanted to melt into him. She wanted to be a part of him forever.

When he anchored his heavy leg against hers Isabella knew Antonio was about to take all control away from her. She was tempted to be swept away one last time, but today she wanted to focus all her love and attention on Antonio.

Isabella moved swiftly and escaped Antonio's embrace. Before he could protest or pin her down she straddled his hips. His hands fell on her waist, his fingers digging into her skin as she slowly sank down on his erection.

She closed her eyes as Antonio's groan echoed around her. Hot pleasure bloomed inside her, pressing heavily until she thought every inch of her skin would blister. She tentatively rolled her hips and was immediately rewarded with a deep thrust from Antonio.

He gained a firmer hold on her hips and lifted her slightly before he bucked hard against her. White-hot sensations rippled through her center, zooming to the top of her head and the soles of her feet.

She rocked her hips faster, compelled to follow an elemental rhythm. She couldn't get enough of Antonio writhing underneath her. She felt like she was harnessing his power and making it hers. No, she realized as she swiped her hair from her eyes. She was making Antonio hers.

He sat up and her eyes were level with his. Antonio guided her hips to counter each savage thrust. She placed her hands on his jaw and kissed his mouth.

"I love you so much, Antonio," she said against his lips.

His fingers bit into her skin as he ground his mouth

against hers. She matched his raw passion with every kiss, every touch and roll of her hips. The need clawed inside her, stripping her control to ribbons. She arched her spine and tilted her head back just as a ferocious climax screamed through her. Her body clenched, her mind went blank and her skin went hot and cold. Antonio burrowed his face against her breasts, his stubble rasping against her as he let out a hoarse cry of triumph.

Time stood still for Isabella. She wanted to hold on to this moment but it was already slipping away. She clung to Antonio as he guided her back onto the mattress. She curled up next to him and pressed her face against his sweat-slicked chest. She inhaled his scent and closed her eyes.

This was how she wanted to end their affair. No tears, no drama. This was how she needed to say goodbye.

But she had to say it one more time, even if Antonio's breathing indicated he was falling back to sleep. She had to do it now because she wouldn't get another chance.

Isabella looked up at Antonio. His eyes were closed and his features were softened in sleep. "I love you, Antonio," she whispered. "I will always love you."

Hours later, Isabella stood on Antonio's balcony which overlooked Rome. The November breeze was crisp but she didn't go back inside. Her mood was quiet and reflective as she waited for Antonio to finish his phone call and leave his study. She knew he was a busy and important man, but she resented how his business intruded. She didn't want to share Antonio's time and attention while they were leaving for the airport.

Isabella glanced down at her clothes, wishing she had something sleek and sophisticated to wear. Something glamorous that he'd always remember instead of her usual jeans and T-shirt. The sweater did nothing to add to her appearance. It was black, bulky, and it hid her baby bump.

She absently rubbed her belly, excited and nervous about her growing baby. The changes in her body were a physical reminder that it was time to move on. She had been greedy and stayed longer than she should. She didn't want to outstay her welcome and ruin these memories.

"Bella, you must be freezing," Antonio said as he stepped onto the balcony. "What are you doing out here?"

"I just wanted one more look," she said. To her horror, she felt her eyes water and her throat constrict with emotion.

Isabella ducked her head and reached for her backpack. She tried to focus on something else and keep her hands busy. She checked once again that she had her passport, ticket and money. As she was about to put them away something caught her notice.

"Antonio?" Isabella frowned as she read the printout in her hand. She straightened to her full height and looked at him. She tried not to think how masculine and powerful he looked in his dark suit and tie. "Is this a first-class ticket?"

"Yes," he answered abstractedly as he looped a wayward strand of her hair behind her ear. His fingertips brushed her throat and lingered.

Isabella took a step away as dread settled in her stomach. That had to have cost thousands of dollars.

Money she didn't have yet. Money she'd need for her baby. "You shouldn't have done that," she admonished in a hushed tone.

He shrugged and reached for her free hand, slid his fingers between hers. "You wouldn't accept my private plane," he reminded her as his thumb caressed her skin.

"I can't accept it, Antonio." It was going to take a long time before she would have the money from Giovanni's will. There were strict rules about how she could spend the money. She could use it to raise her baby but not repay a personal debt. "It's going to take me forever to pay off this ticket."

"I don't want you to repay me." He raised her hand to his mouth and pressed his lips against her knuckles.

She sighed and rested her head against his shoulder. It was tempting to accept his offer. She was going to be a poor student for a while. She needed all the help she could get. But she'd made a deal and she wanted to honor it. "It's too expensive."

His hand tightened against hers. Isabella flinched and lifted her head to look at him. His expression was closed and she couldn't tell what he was thinking.

"Then don't use it," he said.

Isabella blinked and gave him a small smile. "And do what instead? Swim my way back to Los Angeles?" she asked lightly.

She felt the nervous energy simmering in Antonio as he braced his shoulders. "You could stay."

She stared at Antonio's profile. He wasn't looking at her but she saw the ruddy streaks against his cheekbones and the tension in his jaw. If she didn't know any better she'd think he was feeling shy.

Stay? Hope blossomed through her body. She tried

to tamp down her growing excitement. She could have misunderstood his offer, but was he offering something more than affair? More than a duty to her and her child?

"Here? With you?" she clarified, her breath lodging in her throat.

"Yes." He risked a glance in her direction. "If that's what you want."

Antonio appeared vulnerable. His muscles were stiff and his dark eyes were hooded. He was reaching out, uncertain of her answer. He knew she loved him, but he wasn't sure if she would make the same sacrifices again.

She shouldn't. She had put her life on hold to be with him and then, when he had dumped her, she'd had nothing. Working in that café, with no money or opportunities, she'd sworn she would not put herself in that situation again. She would protect herself and not rely on any man. Especially not Antonio, who had the power to destroy her.

So why was she even considering his offer? Hadn't she learned anything? But this time it was different. This was not a vacation fling or an affair. Or was it?

Her chest squeezed with dismay. He had asked her to stay—something she'd needed to hear after he'd kicked her out all those months ago—but he hadn't said that he loved her. He wasn't offering anything more.

Isabella felt tears burn her eyes. "I want to," she said in a raspy voice. "But I can't."

Antonio closed his eyes briefly. His throat tightened as he swallowed. "Why not?"

She pressed her hand against his cheek. Oh, how she wished she didn't have to reject him. It hurt her just as much as it hurt him. "It's complicated."

He placed his hand on hers, trapping her against

him as he opened his eyes and held her gaze. "It's actually very simple. I want to be with you. You want to be with me."

Was that enough? It hadn't been enough last time. And this time she had a baby to consider. She needed more. She needed to know that he was going to be with her no matter what.

"You shouldn't make big changes when you're still in mourning," Isabella decided. She had learned that after her mother's death. Antonio had had a complicated relationship with his brother and needed time to come to terms with Giovanni's death.

"You think I'm doing this out of grief?" His eyes glittered with annoyance. "Do you believe that because I no longer have my brother I feel alone in the world?"

"Well, yes. It's possible." Isabella hoped it wasn't. She wanted to believe that the bond they shared was deep and powerful, but knew his feelings might only be temporary. She wasn't going to stay only to discover that Antonio had made this choice because he was bereaved.

"I'm not trying to fill a void," he said, his voice low and rough. "If anything I've realized how I want to spend the rest of my life. I want to spend it with you."

Isabella froze. Had he really said that or was she hearing what she wanted to hear? She was almost too scared to move. "What are you saying?"

"I love you, Isabella." He turned his head and pressed his mouth against the palm of her hand. "I want to be with you. Always."

Isabella inhaled a jagged breath. *He loved her.* She wanted to fling herself into his arms but something was holding her back. She was scared to trust his words. Scared to find out that her idea of love wasn't his.

"This is moving too fast." She snatched her hand away from him and clenched her fists, her pulse skipping erratically. "I…I need to think about this."

Antonio moved closer. His harsh features were sharp and there was a predatory gleam in his eyes. He didn't like her answer and was determined to make her yield. "What's there to think about? Why do you need to think about it in Los Angeles instead of here with me?"

"I…. It's just that…"

There was an apologetic knock on the balcony door. Isabella whirled around and saw the housekeeper standing in the doorway. She was wringing her hands in her starched apron.

"I'm sorry to interrupt," Martina said, trying not to make eye contact, "but your mother is here, sir."

Antonio closed his eyes and took a deep breath. He didn't hide the displeasure on his face as he held his temper firmly in check.

"Why is your mother here?" Isabella said. She couldn't imagine that Maria wanted to see her off to the airport. She had not spoken to Maria since the day she had been invited for tea.

"I don't know," he said as he reluctantly moved away. "I'll be right back."

She didn't say anything as she watched him leave. Antonio loved her and wanted her to stay. But as what? His girlfriend? His mistress? His wife?

And would he love her child?

She tried to imagine Antonio as a father.

He would be loving and affectionate. She knew that deep in her bones. He would be firm but gentle. He wouldn't make the same mistakes as his own parents. He would encourage and support his child no matter what challenges they faced. Antonio would give his child unconditional love, but would he give it to *her*?

Her opinion was swift. Yes, he would love her child. She didn't know why she was even questioning it. Antonio was already a part of her baby's life. He'd been there every step of the way.

Isabella felt as if a weight had been lifted off her. She was willing to take the risk and tell Antonio that she'd stay. She knew they could be a family. She didn't need to hear a marriage proposal. She wanted one, but she didn't need it to make her decision. Antonio loved her and cared about her baby. He proved it every day.

They could have a wonderful future together, Isabella thought as she grabbed her backpack and strode across the balcony. She was prepared to live and love boldly, without a safety net.

Isabella stepped into the apartment but didn't see Antonio or his mother. She heard voices coming from the study and hesitated. She didn't really want to see Maria Rossi. The woman intimidated her. But she was Antonio's mother and the grandmother of her child. Isabella gritted her teeth and threw back her shoulders before marching over to the study.

"Why is she leaving?" Isabella heard Maria ask in Italian. "You were supposed to convince her to stay."

"She hasn't left yet," Antonio replied. "And she can always come back."

"Yes, yes, yes. She *says* she'll visit so the child can know his heritage and his family, but there's no guarantee."

Isabella frowned as she listened by the study door.

Did Maria still think she would prevent her from know-ing her grandchild? That she had no intention of keep-ing in contact?

Isabella was about to step into the study, but froze mid-step when she heard Maria's next words.

"You were supposed to marry her and adopt the baby so we can gain full control of the Rossi shares." Maria's tone was sharp. "What happened?"

Isabella went cold. Antonio had said he wanted her. That he wanted to look after the baby. That he loved her. Her stomach made a sickening twist. It had all been lies.

"I *will* marry Isabella," Antonio told his mother.

His confident tone scraped at Isabella. There was no question that she would have accepted his proposal. Hell, she would have jumped at the offer with pathetic eagerness. She loved him and had been about to give up everything again to be with him.

"And adopt the baby?" Maria asked.

Isabella gasped as pain ricocheted in her chest. She clasped her shaky hand against her mouth. How could Antonio have devised such a diabolical plan? And how could she have fallen for it so easily?

She should have known he wasn't going to accept Giovanni's baby into his heart. This was why he'd said he wanted to take care of them and show full support. So down the line he could win full custody of Gio's child.

Isabella pressed her hand against the wall as her knees threatened to buckle. It would have worked. If she had married Antonio she would have wanted him to adopt the baby. She would have encouraged it!

And he would have stolen her child away from her. The cold-hearted bastard.

Isabella thrust out her chin and took a deep breath. She wasn't going to let that happen. She didn't care that Maria intimidated her or that Antonio wielded enormous power. She would protect her child from the Rossi family.

Isabella stepped into the study, prepared for battle.

CHAPTER FOURTEEN

When Antonio saw Isabella enter the study a sense of dread shrouded him and weighed heavily on his shoulders. Isabella's complexion was pale and her posture was rigid. Her hands were clenched at her sides but it was her eyes that gave her away. She looked wounded. He knew she'd heard his damning words.

Antonio prided himself on his quick thinking. He was usually a man of action. Yet at this moment he couldn't move. His mind went blank as blinding panic flared inside him. There was no way he could recover from this.

His mother frowned as she watched his expression transform from annoyance to caution. She turned to the door and saw Isabella. Maria immediately pasted on a polite smile and acted as if nothing had been said. After years of gossiping and backbiting with her social circle Maria Rossi wasn't flustered. She was in her element. The only sign that she was taken by surprise was the way she fiddled with her pearl necklace.

"Isabella," his mother greeted her in English. "I wanted to see you before you left for America. I hope you will return soon."

"I have no intention of coming back," Isabella replied in Italian, "I am not giving you the opportunity to steal my child."

Maria flinched and her face went a mottled red. Her movements were choppy as she turned his attention to Antonio. "You told me she didn't speak Italian," she hissed.

"I said no such thing," Antonio replied, his gaze firmly on Isabella's trembling jaw. "Gio probably gave you that impression but he was wrong."

Unfortunately for him. How could he convince Isabella that he had abandoned his plans? Would she believe that now he really wanted to marry her and adopt her child? No. She would never trust his motivations. He didn't blame her.

"Isabella—" his mother began, but faltered to a stop as Isabella glared at her.

"Mother, I think it would be best if you left. Bella and I need to talk."

Maria looked uncertain as she glanced at Isabella and then back at him. She was very aware of Isabella's unpredictable anger quivering in the air.

"I don't think that would be wise."

Antonio sighed softly. Of all the times his mother chose now to give him support. She knew she'd made a big mistake, and he appreciated her need to back him up, but he didn't need her here. This was between him and Isabella. "Please?"

Maria's shoulders sagged in defeat. She grabbed her purse from his desk, patted her chignon to make sure every hair was in place, and gave Isabella a wide berth as she walked out of the study.

Antonio held Isabella's furious gaze but they didn't exchange a word. The moment they heard his mother leave the apartment and shut the door Isabella took an angry step forward.

"Was *anything* we shared true?" Her tone was low and fierce. "Or was it all a lie?"

Antonio saw the pain and the rage in her eyes. He wanted to wrap his arms around her, hold her close and take the hurt from her. He knew how she felt. He had wrestled with that very question when he'd thought she had cheated on him. It ate away at him to the point where he didn't think he would be whole again.

"You still believe I cheated on you," she said, her eyes narrowing into slits. "You told me you believed me so I would get closer to you."

"No, I believe you." She had been innocent, and he had renewed this affair under false pretenses. She would never forgive him and he had to live with the fact that he'd ruined their second chance for happiness.

"I don't think so. You will say anything to get what you want. You'd even go so far as to marry me if it means getting control of the family fortune. Why, you'd even say you love me when you can't stand the sight of me."

"That's not true." Antonio moved and stood in front of her. "I do love you. You don't have to question that. I have proved it every day since we got back together."

"No, you've proved that you're a very good actor. You've pretended to look after me when what you were really doing was looking after your own interests." Her hand shook with fury as she pointed accusingly at him. "You said you wanted to give me everything, but once you'd got what you wanted you would have taken it all away."

Antonio reared back as if he'd been hit. How could

she say that? Did she think him that low? "I would never do that and you know it."

"I thought I knew you, but obviously I don't." She shook her head in disgust. "I was thrilled when you finally opened up to me, but that was part of the plan, wasn't it? Were the stories even true?"

"Of course they were." Her accusations stung. He had shared those memories knowing he could trust them to Isabella. "I told you things I haven't told anyone else."

She wasn't listening. "But the *pièce de resistance* of your plan was pure genius," she declared with the sweep of her hand. "Proving that you could be a good father to my child. Only it was all a show."

"No, it wasn't," he said through clenched teeth.

"You even got your friends involved so that you could demonstrate how good you are with children. And I fell for it!"

"That's not true," he insisted. "I didn't fake anything with my friends. I adore those kids and you have no right to question that."

She thrust out her chin. "And *you* had no right seducing me," she said in a growl, her eyes flashing with ferocious anger. "Making me believe that you wanted a second chance. I knew you wanted to control my child's inheritance but I didn't think you'd try to take my child as well."

"That was not my intention." Antonio said coldly. He needed his words to pierce through her tumultuous emotions. "I would never separate you from your child."

"I heard what your mother said."

"Yes, my mother said it. Not me."

"Then what *was* your plan?" she asked, placing her fists on her hips. "I know you had one. You set it in motion when you found me at that café. Why would you come looking for me when you could have had someone else do the job?"

Antonio couldn't deny it. Isabella knew him well. That hadn't been a disadvantage in the past. She'd known his good and bad sides and still fallen in love with him. He had destroyed that love once before but this was different. There was no hope after this.

He wanted to lie. He should lie if he wanted to save what they had together. But he couldn't. It was time he owned up to his plan. Isabella deserved to know the truth and understand what he was capable of doing.

"I didn't know why Gio named you in the will. I thought it was to remind me of what he could steal away from me—you *and* my birthright. I wasn't going to let that happen and I planned to take back the power he'd given you."

She crossed her arms and glared at him. "I've already figured that out. What did you plan to do?"

Antonio looked away guiltily. Maybe it was best if he didn't tell her *everything*.

"Oh, my God," Isabella whispered and dropped her hands to her sides. "You were going to seduce me so I would give up my child's claim to the Rossi fortune."

Isabella took a cautious step back as she realized Antonio's plan. *That* was why he'd wanted more than a one-night stand. *That* was why he had been insistent on sharing his bed. It wasn't because he found her irresistible. He had been manufacturing emotional intimacy before he moved in for the kill.

She blanched as she remembered how open and trusting she had been in Antonio's arms. "Giovanni said you wouldn't touch me once you found out I was pregnant with his child," she said in a broken whisper. "I thought that was true until you kissed me...." She had thought Antonio couldn't help himself despite everything that happened between them.

"I always wanted you," he confessed. "Even when I thought you were sleeping with my brother. I can't stop wanting you."

His raw tone revealed how much he loved *and* hated the power she had over him. She knew the feeling. Antonio was her weakness, her vice. Only he'd used it against her.

"I knew early on that you weren't going to accept any financial settlement," Antonio said. "I *didn't* have sex with you to regain power over the family fortune. I made love to you because I wanted to be with you."

Despite the anger and pain pouring through her, Isabella wanted to believe him. And that scared her. She wanted desperately to believe that their relationship was as straightforward as it had been in the beginning. It hurt even to think about how beautifully simple their love affair had been.

Pain seeped into her bones. Her limbs felt heavy and she wanted to lean against the nearest wall before sliding down to the floor. She refrained from wrapping her arms around her middle or curling into a protective ball. She would not show any weakness or tears in front of this man. He would use her feelings to his advantage, just as he'd used her attraction and seduced her back into his bed.

"So," she said, her voice rough as her throat tightened, "you had to go with a Plan B. You needed to marry me. That would have been very difficult for you.

Antonio Rossi making a commitment? Especially to a nobody."

"I have never thought of you as a nobody."

"No, you saw me as the woman pregnant with the Rossi heir. That's the only reason you'd consider marrying me. You certainly weren't thinking that when we were together the first time."

Antonio shoved his hand in her dark, thick hair. "I admit that my reason for restarting our affair wasn't honest, but that changed. *I* changed."

Isabella snorted. "How convenient."

He grabbed her arms and forced her to face him. She met his gaze head-on. She wasn't afraid. She wasn't going to back down. Nothing he said or did could make her feel any worse.

"I want a future with you, Bella. When you came back into my life I knew that I couldn't let you go. It isn't about the money or the baby. It's about *us*."

Isabella slowly raised her hands and flattened them on his solid chest. She felt the strong beat of his heart. Antonio was telling her everything she needed to hear. Just like he had week after week. And somehow she was supposed to believe that the lies had become the truth?

Isabella pushed him away and he reluctantly let go of her arms.

"You have to believe me," Antonio said. "I don't know how to prove it to you. How can I show you how much I love you?"

"You can't." It was over. She couldn't make it work by clinging on to him, on to the promise of this relationship. Isabella turned around and headed for the door. She had to get out of here before she found a reason not to.

"I'm not going to let you walk out of my life again," he warned her.

"Yes, you are," she said hoarsely as emotion clawed at her throat. She didn't dare face him. "Last time you dumped me. This time I'm making a run for it."

She felt Antonio follow her. Isabella wanted to hurry and hide. She had to get out before her resolve weakened. Before she allowed herself to believe anything he said. She grabbed her backpack and swung it over her shoulders. Ducking her head and keeping her eyes straight ahead, she reached the front door in record time.

"We are a part of each other's lives," Antonio said. "You can't shut me out."

"Antonio, soon you will be a distant memory. Ancient history." She wrenched the door open. "A cautionary tale I'll share with my daughter."

"You're forgetting something."

Antonio's harsh voice was right behind her. She felt him tower over her, inhaled his scent that invaded her senses.

"We share power over the Rossi empire. That means we'll have to work together. We will be in constant contact."

Isabella's hand flexed on the doorknob. What he said was true. Antonio would be part of her life from now on. She would need to deal with him on a daily basis. She would have to watch from the sidelines as he got on with his life while she was once again picking up the pieces.

"I'll give you power of attorney, or whatever they call it," she said impulsively. "You can make all the decisions without having to discuss it with me."

"That's not how it works and it's not what I want."

Antonio cupped his hand over her shoulders and turned her around. "You can't throw me out of your life that easily."

Why not? He'd done it to her and he would have done it again. "I don't want to have anything to with you or the Rossi business."

"Too bad. I'm going to be with you every step of the way whether you like it or not. You're angry with me now—"

"Angry? Try furious. Try homicidal."

"But soon you will realize that everything we shared was true. That I wasn't pretending and that I am committed to you and the baby."

"I can't take that chance." She had taken too many risks only to have them blow up in her face. She couldn't trust Antonio at his word only to have him try to take her child away.

There was only one way she could protect her baby and her future. Her heart started to pound and she felt her skin flush. The idea was crazy, and she should think it through, but it was the only way she would get Antonio out of her life for good.

"I'm giving up my child's claim to the Rossi fortune," she said in a rush. "I don't want the shares or anything. It's all yours."

Antonio's eyes widened and his hands tightened on her shoulders. "Are you crazy? What are you talking about?"

She pulled away from him. "When I get back to Los Angeles I will have a lawyer draw up the paperwork. All the money, all the shares—everything will belong to you."

"You can't do this."

"Yes, I can," she said defiantly. The more she thought about it, the more she knew it was the right decision. This was the only way she'd be free.

"You can't give away a fortune. What about your child? It should belong to him. This is part of who he is."

It didn't have to be. "I don't want him to know anything about his heritage or his family. I need to protect him from becoming someone like Giovanni or you."

Antonio's eyes flashed with anger. "Bella, I won't let you do this. You're making a big mistake."

"Why are you fighting me, Antonio?" she asked as she crossed the threshold. "You're getting everything you want without making any sacrifice."

"Not everything," he told her. "I want *you*."

"Don't worry, Antonio," she said as she walked away. "I'm sure the feeling is temporary."

CHAPTER FIFTEEN

Four months later

ISABELLA gripped onto the wall railing and paused. She was shaky and she felt sweat bead on her forehead. She had tried to do too much, determined to heal quickly after the Caesarean. After all, she was going home alone with her baby girl in a couple of hours. She needed to be able to move.

Glancing around the busy maternity ward, she saw that her room was at the end of the hall. Isabella was tempted to give up and ask for a wheelchair, but she wasn't a quitter. She had become a fighter. There'd been plenty of days when she'd survived on grit alone.

After she had returned to California she'd ignored the desire to curl up in a ball and cry. She'd had to get on with her life and take care of her baby. It had not been easy, but she now had a tiny apartment, a few friends, and a job at an art gallery. Soon she would return to college and complete her art history degree.

Now if only she could erase Antonio from her mind... If she could stop dreaming about him, that would be great. Those dreams reminded her of what she had lost, what she would never have again. One day she would be rid of the empty hollowness inside her, but until then she needed to stop thinking about the past and focus on the future.

When she stepped into her room Isabella swore she would never take walking for granted again. All she wanted to do was get back into bed and rest. Intent on putting one foot in front of the other, she didn't realize she had a visitor.

"Bella."

Only one person called her that. Isabella glanced up, the movement so sharp and sudden that she almost lost her balance. She flattened her hand on the wall when she saw Antonio standing by the window.

Her heart did a slow and painful flip as she greedily took in the sight of him. She must be imagining things. Isabella blinked but the vision of Antonio didn't go away. He looked exactly as he had when she'd left him. Powerful, harsh and incredibly sexy. His scowl and the tailored business suit made him even more intimidating.

Isabella knew she looked a mess, with her limp hair and voluminous hospital gown. "What are you doing here?" she asked weakly.

"I'm here for you."

Damn, those words still sent a shiver of excitement down her spine. Antonio was always going to have this effect on her. It wasn't fair. She didn't need this in her life. She didn't need *him*.

"You need to leave." She wished she could leave, but she knew she wouldn't get far. Gathering all the strength she could muster, Isabella pushed one foot in front of the other. She needed to get to the bed before she collapsed.

Antonio frowned as he saw her awkward gait and

was suddenly at her side. "Let me help you," he offered as he gently placed a hand on her back.

She would have shrugged him off if she'd trusted her balance a little more. "I can do it myself. I need the practice," she insisted.

Antonio dropped his hand but walked with her to the bed. The journey was slow and painful, and she knew Antonio was tempted to pick her up and carry her. She increased her speed, finding it easier to walk having someone nearby. Antonio might have betrayed her, but she knew he wouldn't let her fall.

Once she'd sat on the bed Isabella gave a sigh of relief. She lay down, wincing and hissing a breath between her clenched teeth. Antonio didn't say anything as he pulled the blanket over her and tucked her in.

She didn't want his kindness. She might read too much into the gesture. "Now tell me why you're here," Isabella said as she sank into her pillow.

"I saw your daughter," Antonio said, his voice low and husky. "She's beautiful."

Antonio had already seen Chiara? She stiffened as the need to protect her child crashed through her like violent wave. She hadn't been prepared for that. She hadn't thought Antonio would be interested.

"She looks like her father."

He nodded. "Yes, she does. But I also see a lot of you in her."

She glanced at his face, but Antonio showed no sign of resentment. He had simply stated a matter of fact. It was as if Chiara's parentage didn't bother him. How was that possible? Was she seeing what she wanted to see?

Isabella closed her eyes. "Antonio, I'm really not up for visitors."

"You haven't been for four months," he said in a growl.

She wouldn't apologize for that. The first time he'd called her Isabella had recognized the number and hadn't picked up. She had spent the rest of the day alternating between tears and stone-cold anger. But she'd also known that she wanted to talk to Antonio, hold on to that connection. And that had scared her. How could she move on if she still felt like that?

"I've been busy," she said. "My life has gone through a lot of transitions."

"I tried to contact you."

"Yeah, I know." She had blocked his calls and texts, deleted his e-mails without opening them, and trashed the flower bouquets that had appeared on her desk at work. Anything related to her child's inheritance had been directed to her lawyer, whom she could barely afford. She had to avoid anything that reminded her of Antonio.

She'd wanted to give him full power over the Rossi shares, but he had refused to accept it. He still acted as if he needed her approval over every decision. Isabella wasn't sure why he was trying to include her in everything. He didn't need to keep in contact with her. He no longer had to pretend that he could love her and her child.

Disappointment coiled tightly in her chest. So, if he had everything he wanted, why was he here? Today of all days? She didn't want to talk to Antonio about her baby.

"I don't have the money yet to pay you back for the ticket," she said in a rush. "We'll have to make a payment plan. It'll take a while because—"

"I don't want your money. That ticket was a gift," he interrupted, annoyed. "I'm here because I heard you were in labor. Unfortunately I didn't get here in time. If I had I would have found you better accommodations."

She opened her eyes and looked around the room. It was clean, simple and private. It was better than she had hoped. What more could she possibly want? "This is fine. I won't be here for much longer. They are sending me home in a couple of hours."

Outrage flickered in his dark eyes. "That is unacceptable. You can barely walk. I will speak to the doctors immediately."

"Wait a second." She weakly lifted her hand as she realized what he had said a few moments ago. "How did you know I was in labor? Are you having me watched?"

"Of course. I was worried about you. I remember that room you had over the café when I found you." He suppressed his shudder of distaste. "I didn't want that to happen again."

"I don't like being watched or followed," she told him. "I can take care of myself. I don't need your help."

"Then why did you put me down as emergency contact on your medical forms? Why did you make me the guardian to Chiara if anything happened to you?"

Isabella cringed. She had wrestled with that choice. She could have named a friend, but in the end she'd wanted Antonio to look after Chiara. "You know about that?"

"I do." Triumph flared in his eyes. "You know deep down that I would take care of you and the baby. That I would treat your daughter as my own."

She felt the heat crawl up her neck. "You shouldn't

read anything into those decisions. I was required to give a name."

"And you chose mine. Because you know I want to be here. That I want to help."

He said that now, but how long would it last? "No, you don't want to help. Not unless you get something in return. I can't figure out your ulterior motive, but I know you have one."

Antonio sighed. "I regret that. At the time I made promises that I wasn't planning to keep."

"Just as I expected."

He shoved his hand through his hair. "But that changed once we were back together. I started to believe that this was our second chance. I wasn't thinking about gaining control as much as I was thinking about recapturing what we'd once shared."

"And when did that change of heart happen?" Isabella asked, her voice filled with skepticism.

"When you handed me the sonogram." Antonio said, his voice fading as he recalled that moment. "I looked at it and I didn't see the baby as an obstacle or a sign of betrayal. I saw this small, innocent child that was part of *you*. And I knew I wanted to go on this journey with you."

Isabella stared at him as the sincerity in his voice tugged at her. She wanted to believe him, but what if this was another act? How could she trust her instincts when he had played her so well before?

Antonio cleared his throat and awkwardly rubbed the back of his neck. "Once I found where you had gone I tried to reach out. I wanted to talk to you."

"You were very persistent."

Antonio reached out and covered her hand with his.

"I now know how you must have felt when I kicked you out. I was desperate and out of control. No matter how hard I tried, you wouldn't talk to me."

"I still don't want to talk to you." As much as she wanted to hold onto his hand, she purposely removed her fingers from his grasp.

"I understand, but I should have been here. You shouldn't have gone through this alone."

"I wasn't alone. I have friends." Friends who would adore her and her baby, no matter what her shortcomings were.

"Yes, I know," he said, the corner of his mouth slanting up in a smile. "They gathered around you in a protective circle. My security team could take a few lessons from them."

"Considering our history," Isabella said gently, "it's better if I don't accept your help."

"No, it's not." Antonio leaned over Isabella, bracing his arms on the bedrails. "If you don't want me by your side then I'll help you behind the scenes. I want to give you every opportunity to finish your college degree. I will support your dreams and goals. I'm not asking for your permission, Bella. I'm doing this because I want to."

Isabella fought back the hope that pressed against her chest. "And Chiara?"

"I want to take you and Chiara back to Rome," Antonio replied.

She frowned. "Why would you do that?"

"So we can be a family." Antonio leaned in closer. "These months have been hell, knowing that I've lost you again."

Family. There was that word again. It was as if he

knew her weakness and understood her deepest desire. "You can't just walk in here and expect me to change my life again so we can have another affair. My situation has changed. I have a child I need to think about."

"I said a family." Antonio's gaze held her immobile. "I want us to get married."

Married?

"You don't need to marry me," she said, her eyes wide and her heart starting to pound. "I offered you full control of the Rossi shares."

"I love you."

His sincerity tugged at her heart.

"And I know you love me."

"I… I…" She couldn't deny it. She loved Antonio and wanted to be with him—but love wasn't enough.

"Marry me, Bella." He rested his forehead against hers. "I want to be with you and Chiara. Always."

She slowly exhaled and looked away. There had to be another reason. An ulterior motive. Why would he want her as his wife if she didn't meet any of his requirements?

"No," she whispered.

Antonio froze. "Excuse me?"

"I'm sorry, Antonio. I can't marry you."

Antonio drew back. Isabella had said no. *No.* The word sliced through him like a knife. He gripped the bedrail as hurt bled through him. Had he ruined what they'd shared? Was it beyond repair?

He wouldn't accept that. They loved each other and they would get through this. He needed Isabella. His life was dark and empty without her and he didn't want to go through another day apart from her.

He should have come for her earlier. Antonio bowed his head with regret. He had stayed in Rome to fix the financial mess his brother had left. Not only had Gio been deeply in debt, but the Rossi family fortune was at stake. If Antonio hadn't stepped in Chiara would have inherited nothing.

And he had also stayed in Rome to make some changes in his life. He'd scaled back on his work significantly so his focus could be on his family life. He'd also found a house that would be perfect for raising children. Now that he had suffered twice from being separated from Isabella, he didn't want to miss out on another moment.

But Isabella didn't see it that way. She didn't want him to be a part of her life.

A horrible thought occurred to him. His stomach twisted with dread as he asked, "Do you want to be with me?"

"Yes," Isabella said. She wiped the tears from her eyes and sniffled. "But it's not possible."

"Of course it is," he insisted as relief poured through him. "We are free to get married. I don't want anyone but you. I know you haven't dated anyone since you were with me. There is no one holding us back."

"I don't trust you," she said. "You say everything I want to hear, but you did that before and it was all lies."

He took a step back as hurt seeped into him. "It wasn't all lies."

"You showed interest and concern because you wanted control of the money. What do you want from me now?"

"I wasn't faking it."

"Why are you still around?" Isabella asked. "I tried

to transfer my interest in the Rossi empire but you won't sign the paperwork. Just take it. You'd have full control with my blessing."

"I don't want your blessing," he said in a growl. "I want you and the baby."

"That doesn't make sense. I would not make you a good wife. I don't have the right background, the right—"

"You *are* good for me," he insisted. "You're generous and affectionate. You're bold and adventurous. You nurture and protect the ones you love. You love ferociously and you are deeply loyal."

"There's nothing special about that."

"You have no idea how rare that is." He crossed his arms and began to pace the room. "I know what it's like to grow up in a family and feel like an outsider. I'm not going to let that happen to Chiara. She won't have to earn my love or my affection. She already has it."

"How can she have it?" she threw back at him angrily. "You think I was being unfaithful to you when she was conceived."

"I did at first. I can't deny it." He rubbed his hands over his face. "It destroyed me. But that was when I thought you had cheated on me. I don't care that she's Giovanni's daughter or even that she's a Rossi. She is *your* child and I want to raise her with you."

"That doesn't change anything," she said slowly, as if she'd been taken by surprise. "I won't marry you."

"I won't stop asking," he said as he stalked back to the bed, unable to hide his frustration. "I am bound to you whether or not we're married."

"And if I keep refusing?"

"That won't change how I feel. You walked away

from me but I kept my commitment to you. I will make sure you and the baby are getting the best care," he confessed. "I will always take care of you and Chiara even if we don't marry. Never question that."

He didn't know how he could prove his love for her and Chiara. He had demonstrated it when they had been together, but those actions had been tainted with his original plan. If Isabella returned to him she'd been taking a great leap of faith.

"I'm asking you to trust me," he said as he took her hand again. This time she didn't pull away. "I will show you, Bella. You once gave everything to make our relationship work and I have the same commitment to you and Chiara."

"You say that now…"

"I will prove it every day," he vowed. "Starting today. I'm taking you to my hotel and I will look after you and the baby."

She pressed her lips together as she considered his offer. "I'm not sure about this," she said nervously.

It wasn't quite a yes, but she hadn't said no. Antonio smiled triumphantly.

"I'm still not marrying you," Isabella warned him.

"You will," he said as he raised her hand to his lips. "When you trust me. You will."

EPILOGUE

ISABELLA stirred awake and instinctively reached for Antonio. Her fingers brushed against the warm, crumpled bedsheet. She frowned and slowly opened her eyes, her gaze focusing on her hand. The diamonds on her wedding ring caught the faint light and sparkled in the shadowy bedroom.

Propping herself on her elbow, Isabella squinted at the bedside clock and saw that it was a little after three in the morning. She glanced around the large room. The curtains were still pulled back and she saw the Rome skyline glittering in the distance.

"Antonio?" she called out softly, her voice husky with sleep.

She rose from the bed when she didn't receive an answer. Grabbing her discarded nightgown that was lying on the floor in a pool of satin, Isabella slid it over her body. The hem skimmed her thighs.

She tiptoed barefoot out of the bedroom and paused at the threshold when she heard faint whispering. It sounded like Antonio's voice, and it came from the direction of the nursery. Isabella felt a flicker of worry. Had Chiara cried out and she hadn't heard it?

Isabella reached the door to the nursery and peered

inside. She saw Antonio, wearing a dark pair of pajama bottoms slung low on his lean hips. The sight of him gently cradling her fussy baby in his arms made her breath hitch in her throat.

Antonio should look out of place in the pink and green nursery. He was too sexy, his looks too darkly erotic, to sit in a rocking chair. He was known for his power and ruthlessness, but one year-old Chiara had already wrapped him around her tiny finger.

"Chiara, listen to your papa," Antonio said in a hushed, mesmerizing tone to the infant snuggled against his bare muscular chest. "We had an agreement. You are to sleep when the moon is out."

Isabella leaned against the doorframe as she watched her husband and her child. They had an agreement? She bit back a smile. How frequently did Antonio and Chiara have these late-night heart-to-hearts?

It shouldn't surprise her. From the moment she and Chiara had left the hospital Antonio had gotten into the habit of long talks with her daughter. He would encourage Chiara to reach for a toy, he would read the newspaper to her as if it was a children's fairytale, and he would soothe her when she cried loudly during her bath.

"A Rossi always honors his word," he murmured as he stroked the baby's back.

Chiara sighed and her tiny body relaxed against Antonio's chest.

"Remember," Antonio said softly as he laid the baby in her crib, "you get your mama's undivided attention during the day while I'm at work. I get your mama at night."

"Did you ever think," Isabella whispered as she walked into the nursery, "that Chiara gets up in the middle of the night so she can have *your* undivided attention?"

"Then she's a smart girl." He tucked a light blanket around the infant.

Isabella was enamored of the depth of patience and tenderness Antonio demonstrated. He always had words of praise and optimism, whether Chiara had an accomplishment or a setback. She knew Antonio would be a great father.

Antonio turned and Isabella could see his exaggerated scowl in the faint moonlight. "That nightgown looks familiar. Didn't I strip it off you earlier tonight?"

"You did," Isabella said with a smile as sexual excitement bubbled inside her. "I thought I should wear something special for our wedding night, but you ripped it right off me."

"And now you've put it back on?" His voice was low and playful. "You should be punished."

"You need to catch me first." She hurried out the door and got all the way to the hallway before she felt Antonio's arm wrap around her waist. Isabella bit back a squeal as he flattened her spine against his chest.

"I've got you," he said triumphantly against her ear as he pushed the straps of her nightgown past her shoulders. "And I'm not letting go."

She sensed a deeper meaning in his words. The nightgown slid past her hips and onto the floor. She turned and looped her arms around his broad shoulders, the tips of her breasts grazing his chest. "I'm not letting go, either. You can count on that."

* * * * *

Mills & Boon® Hardback

January 2013

ROMANCE

Beholden to the Throne	Carol Marinelli
The Petrelli Heir	Kim Lawrence
Her Little White Lie	Maisey Yates
Her Shameful Secret	Susanna Carr
The Incorrigible Playboy	Emma Darcy
No Longer Forbidden?	Dani Collins
The Enigmatic Greek	Catherine George
The Night That Started It All	Anna Cleary
The Secret Wedding Dress	Ally Blake
Driving Her Crazy	Amy Andrews
The Heir's Proposal	Raye Morgan
The Soldier's Sweetheart	Soraya Lane
The Billionaire's Fair Lady	Barbara Wallace
A Bride for the Maverick Millionaire	Marion Lennox
Take One Arranged Marriage...	Shoma Narayanan
Mad About the Man	Joss Wood
Breaking the Playboy's Rules	Emily Forbes
Hot-Shot Doc Comes to Town	Susan Carlisle

MEDICAL

The Surgeon's Doorstep Baby	Marion Lennox
Dare She Dream of Forever?	Lucy Clark
Craving Her Soldier's Touch	Wendy S. Marcus
Secrets of a Shy Socialite	Wendy S. Marcus

D HB

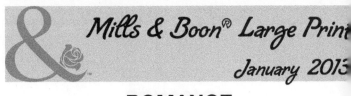

Mills & Boon® Large Print

January 2013

ROMANCE

Unlocking her Innocence	Lynne Graham
Santiago's Command	Kim Lawrence
His Reputation Precedes Him	Carole Mortimer
The Price of Retribution	Sara Craven
The Valtieri Baby	Caroline Anderson
Slow Dance with the Sheriff	Nikki Logan
Bella's Impossible Boss	Michelle Douglas
The Tycoon's Secret Daughter	Susan Meier
Just One Last Night	Helen Brooks
The Greek's Acquisition	Chantelle Shaw
The Husband She Never Knew	Kate Hewitt

HISTORICAL

His Mask of Retribution	Margaret McPhee
How to Disgrace a Lady	Bronwyn Scott
The Captain's Courtesan	Lucy Ashford
Man Behind the Façade	June Francis
The Highlander's Stolen Touch	Terri Brisbin

MEDICAL

Sydney Harbour Hospital: Marco's Temptation	Fiona McArthur
Waking Up With His Runaway Bride	Louisa George
The Legendary Playboy Surgeon	Alison Roberts
Falling for Her Impossible Boss	Alison Roberts
Letting Go With Dr Rodriguez	Fiona Lowe
Dr Tall, Dark...and Dangerous?	Lynne Marshall

1212 GEN STD LP

Mills & Boon® Hardback
February 2013

ROMANCE

old to the Enemy	Sarah Morgan
ncovering the Silveri Secret	Melanie Milburne
artering Her Innocence	Trish Morey
ealing Her Final Card	Jennie Lucas
the Heat of the Spotlight	Kate Hewitt
More Sweet Surrender	Caitlin Crews
ide After Her Fall	Lucy Ellis
ing the Charade	Michelle Conder
e Downfall of a Good Girl	Kimberly Lang
e One That Got Away	Kelly Hunter
r Rocky Mountain Protector	Patricia Thayer
e Billionaire's Baby SOS	Susan Meier
by out of the Blue	Rebecca Winters
llroom to Bride and Groom	Kate Hardy
w To Get Over Your Ex	Nikki Logan
st Like Kids	Jackie Braun
e Brooding Doc's Redemption	Kate Hardy
e Son that Changed his Life	Jennifer Taylor

MEDICAL

Inescapable Temptation	Scarlet Wilson
ealing The Real Dr Robinson	Dianne Drake
e Rebel and Miss Jones	Annie Claydon
allowbrook's Wedding of the Year	Abigail Gordon

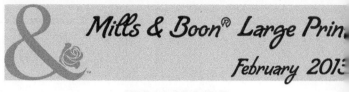

Mills & Boon® Large Print

February 2013

ROMANCE

Banished to the Harem	Carol Marine
Not Just the Greek's Wife	Lucy Monro
A Delicious Deception	Elizabeth Pow
Painted the Other Woman	Julia Jam
Taming the Brooding Cattleman	Marion Lenn
The Rancher's Unexpected Family	Myrna Macken:
Nanny for the Millionaire's Twins	Susan Me
Truth-Or-Date.com	Nina Harring
A Game of Vows	Maisey Ya
A Devil in Disguise	Caitlin Cre
Revelations of the Night Before	Lynn Raye Ha

HISTORICAL

Two Wrongs Make a Marriage	Christine Me
How to Ruin a Reputation	Bronwyn Sc
When Marrying a Duke...	Helen Dick
No Occupation for a Lady	Gail Whit
Tarnished Rose of the Court	Amanda McC

MEDICAL

Sydney Harbour Hospital: Ava's Re-Awakening	Carol Mar
How To Mend A Broken Heart	Amy Andr
Falling for Dr Fearless	Lucy (
The Nurse He Shouldn't Notice	Susan Ca
Every Boy's Dream Dad	Sue Mac
Return of the Rebel Surgeon	Connie